NEW CLUES

to

HARRY POTTER: BOOK 5

Hints from the
Ultimate Unofficial Guide
to the Mysteries of Harry Potter

NEW CLUES

to

HARRY POTTER: BOOK 5

Hints from the
Ultimate Unofficial Guide
to the Mysteries of Harry Potter

Galadriel Waters
assisted by
Prof. Astre Mithrandir
& E. L. Fossa

Wizarding World Press

Published in the United States by Wizarding World Press
8926 N. Greenwood Ave., Vault 133
Niles, IL 60714

Library of Congress Cataloging-in-Publication Data available at the Library of Congress

ISBN 0-9723936-2-5

Printed in the United States of America by TPS (Total Printing Systems), Newton, IL, and
VSI (Visual Systems, Inc.), Milwaukee, WI
Distributed by SCB Distributors, Gardena, CA

Book Cover Design and Layout by Dan Nolte, Graphic Design - www.dannolte.com
Original Book Layout Design by Beth Adams
Original Cover Design and Cover Illustrations by Ron Shulda
Genealogy by Anne Fisher - frelighgenealogy@yahoo.com
Publication Consultant: Nancy Davies
Administration: Terry Felke, Bob Russo, Jack & Shirley Buckley, Tim Miller, Julia and Glenys
Reyes

First Edition, October 31, 2003

Third Printing, February 2, 2004

Fourth Printing, July 31, 2004

*To HP Sleuths who waited patiently while we worked on this guide,
and to J.K. Rowling for luring us into this mystery maze*

Special Thanks to:

Eric "Skully" Scull
Margaret Sebastian

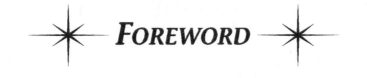

FOREWORD

I have agreed to place my words of wisdom, once again, on the pages of this unofficial Guide to J.K. Rowling's latest wagonful of parchments. Her most recent installment has the touch of Puck in it, and I am having much difficulty deciphering her clever clues, as I seem to have misplaced my own Philological Stone.

I have lately undertaken a new project helping a Druid friend of mine with some construction work, thus, I haven't had much time to follow all the terrible events afflicting modern-day wizards. Nonetheless, I see that young Headmaster (he is only 150) does seem to have things quite under control.

We now know what the Lady Rowling has been doing for three years, and I can assure you it's not snogging in the bathroom (as some have suggested). After reading Book 5, I am thinking of agreeing with those who say we have given her far too much time. I am the first one to advise patience as we wait for a work of art; but, the Lady has gotten so brainy that I can see it is dangerous to give her more than 24 hours to write a novel.

Prior to seeing this New Clues edition, I had thought we were going to be in the dark until sorceress Rowling finished her next bundle of parchments. However, Wizarding World Press has helped me, once again, to become the local sage. As the warnings on this Guide suggest, this Hints-only Guide is not for the lazy or dull-witted, but I can assure you that the clues are really in there to discover, as long as you have your Philological Stone. I am so excited about the latest one I figured out after seeing the hint – that pun in the title of Chapter 24 – "Occlumency." It's as simple as saying it slowly and hearing it phonetically: "Oc...clu...men...cy." You see? It is "A...clue...men...see"!

Uhhh... I don't know if I was supposed to mention that. Well, you get the idea. I've got to get back to this really tricky one in Chapter 10. Now where did I leave that stone...

Merlin

P.S. The video version of Chamber of Secrets gets you thinking too, doesn't it? I will be (quietly) popping by the next movie. See you then!

Message to J. K. Rowling:

We wanted to be able to look ourselves in the mirror (without cracking it) when this is finished, and know that we have done your work justice. Hopefully we've succeeded. So far, we have an almost spotless record (only one oop!), and we are trying to keep it that way. But as you know, even Dumbledore can make mistakes, and we're not nearly in his league.

We have tried to keep in the spirit you intended by giving your fans lots of cool images to reflect on, as they attempt to find the right words and secrets in this second book about your works. You have slipped so many things by us that we are still finding a few twists – even as this is sent down to be permanently inscribed in our latest journal of mysteries. So, we will continue to work on it for at least another calendar year (unless, of course, that prophecy meant 2004 – gulp!).

To be honest, it is hard to keep up with you. We had many sleepless nights staring at the ceiling, as all the strange images you created slithered through our heads while we brainstormed. It took us ages to figure out if those obscurus clues of yours were real or not. We felt like such Neanderthals at times just gaping at the same passage until something finally unraveled in our head and fell at our feet. We were so excited about finding that acrid pink Philological Stone. However, we weren't quite sure how to best describe it (delicately). It will come in very handy for your fans.

For Book 5, we had imagined a Chimaera, an Occamy, or even a killer fungus, but who would have ever thought the worst would come from a froggie female? We don't even think Hagrid would believe that. ☺ Newt Scamander was still very handy this time anyway. Glad Obscurus wasn't too hard to find – had us chasing our tails for awhile, though... Too bad that guy's always so tied up.

We have been working so hard on this fan Guide that we haven't been able to just sit back and read between the lines, so please forgive us if we haven't addressed something important. It has been so much fun to unearth all the little gems you buried in Book 5, and we just can't wait to watch as the pieces all fall together in the heads of your fans!

INTRODUCTION

Welcome back, HP Sleuths, *welcome back!* Thank you for your support. It is because of you that we are able to continue publishing.

J.K. Rowling has done it again! *Harry Potter and the Order of the Phoenix* is not only big and mean, it's a literary tour de force. And it's *pecked...that is...packed* with clues on every page! Harry Potter fans have been given a difficult task if they wish to find and decipher all those clues. In a personal appearance at Royal Albert Hall, J.K.R. put up the challenge when she said: *"I had to put in some things because of what's coming in books 6 and 7 . . . I want you to be able to guess if you've got your wits about you."* Now, what self-respecting HP Sleuth could resist *that* challenge?

Not us. ☺

STOP! BRAINWORK AHEAD

This Guide needs an explanation. Our *New Clues* Guide isn't really a separate book. It should be considered either an addendum to the "Ultimate Unofficial Guide to the Mysteries of Harry Potter (Analysis of Books 1-4)," or a prequel to an "(Analysis of Book 5)." You can think of it as your "scribbler" sleuthing guide. It is not quite the same kind of guide as our first one, since this is a "Hints-only" edition. The purpose of this scribbler sleuthing guide is to help HP Sleuths who are trying to do some of their *own* detective work.

Should you buy this Guide?

⁕ If you want *awesome hints* and want to know *where to look* for the mega clues we have found – this IS the book for you.

⁕ If you want all the answers *now* - this is NOT the book for you.

We will explain.

Did you know it took us almost two years to research and write our analysis of Books 1-4? As Book 5 is approximately the length (in words) of J.K.R.'s first three books combined, it would have taken us at least a year to research and write an analysis of it. We had some other difficult issues. We had considered just updating the original Guide by appending this new section to the end of it and making it longer. But then, that would be unfair to the people who have already bought it.

We banged our heads (Dobby-style) trying to decide how to do it. Some HP Sleuths wanted us to wait until they had time to work out the clues for themselves. Others have been impatiently pelting us with e-owls for our analysis. If we were to give a lot away right now, those people who want to discover the clues for themselves would be miffed. However, those who want answers right away would have to wait about a year for a proper analysis.

What to do? We conjured a win-win solution.

This is a "Hints-only" guide. It includes a trunk's worth of FAQs to explain some of the more complex events that have been bugging you about Book 5. It also points HP Sleuths to the right sections so you know *precisely* where to look for all the mega clues we have spotted, and includes the tools that you need so *you* can find the clues and start solving the mysteries. The HP Hintoscope, WWP Sleuthoscope and Rememberit Quill are all here to help – along with a new, very rare tool called a "Philological Stone." But we *won't* be openly exposing all of the answers in this "New Clues" Guide.

This guide is different in some other ways too. Please note:

NEW SPOILER WARNING!

"New Clues" *doesn't* have a summary of Book 5, and it has a *different* layout — information will be discussed *out of order*. As a Hints guide, it is specifically for HP Sleuths, so we will be assuming that you have already read our first Guide *and most of all,* have finished reading *Harry Potter and the Order of the Phoenix.* That means it is **one big spoiler**! Be forewarned. ☺

We think this Hints guide will be a lot of fun for HP Sleuths. Please keep in mind that it was researched and written in only three (sleepless) months.

Our plan (cross fingers!), is to release *the Ultimate Unofficial Guide to the Mysteries of Harry Potter (Analysis of Book 5)* sometime later. That will have the same format as our original Guide. It will have the answers to these hints, cool observations, and all the Rowlinguistics – along with our popular summary of the mysteries. It also will have our famous "Restricted Area" - containing speculations about what will happen in Book 6 and Beyond. Any additional clues that we have uncovered by then will be included, as well.

If you don't feel like doing the legwork yourself, you can wait until later next year. However, if you just can't sit still until then, dig your HP Sleuth Magical Toolkit out of your trunk and get crackin' on these clues...

WE'RE GOING SNARK HUNTING!

TABLE OF CONTENTS

WWP HELP DESK

FAQs (Frequently Asked Questions)

- ☾ When Should I Read This Guide?
- ☾ Rowlinguistics in Book 5 ...or What Is the "Philological Stone"?
- ☾ Are There Too Many Words in Book 5?
- ☾ Are There Differences Between the UK and U.S. Versions of Book 5?
- ☾ What Is Significant About the Date That Book 5 Was Released?
- ☾ *(Review)* How Reliable Is the Information in This Guide?
- ☾ *(Review)* What Is an Ultimate Unofficial Mystery Guide? *...and What Is an "HP Sleuth"™?*
- ☾ *(Review)* What Is a Septology?

When Should I Read This Guide?

New Clues is for HP Sleuths only! If you have read *Harry Potter and the Order of the Phoenix*, and are ready to ferret for clues and solve the mysteries of Book 5 and Beyond, then this Guide is for you. We are making the assumption that you are familiar with the skills involved in sleuthing a Harry Potter book. We also *highly recommend* that you have read the easily-available school books *Fantastic Beasts and Where to Find Them* and *Quidditch Through the Ages* (see the HP Sleuth Recommended Reading). So, if you haven't, we can't be responsible for glassy looks as you sit staring straight at the clues.

Rowlinguistics in Book 5
...or What Is the "Philological Stone"?

Not only have the reading level and plot line become more advanced in Book 5, but the clues have become far more sophisticated. By Book 7, we may need some NEWT-level spells to decipher all of them! One of the reasons for this new degree of difficulty is J.K.R.'s use of wordplay. In previous books, the Rowlinguistics (J.K.R.'s coined words) generally consisted of words and phrases from mythology, other languages and Olde English that J.K.R. used verbatim ("vol de mort," "dumbledore"), or puns. Sometimes she put a little twist on the spelling, homophone-style, just to give us a bit of a challenge in tracing the words ("Knockturn Alley" = *nocturnally*).

However, just as Harry's personality has become more complex in Book 5 (you may call it multiplexed), the literary tricks J.K.R. has hiding up her sleeve have also become far more intricate. The wordplay that she draws from most often now includes metonyms, homonyms/homophones, malapropisms, portmanteau words, and even baby talk! Depending on how they are implemented, the portmanteau words can be the most difficult.

The way a portmanteau word works is to combine 2 or more words into one so that it sort of looks a little like each word, but not like anything at all. That technique was made famous by Lewis Carroll in his *Alice in Wonderland* stories. As Lewis Carroll explained it:

> *"... take the two words 'fuming' and 'furious.' Make up your mind that you will say both words, but leave it unsettled which you will say first. Now open your mouth and speak. If your thoughts incline ever so little towards 'fuming,' you will say 'fuming-furious;' if they turn, by even a hair's breadth, towards 'furious,' you will say 'furious-fuming;' but if you have the rarest of gifts, a perfectly balanced mind, you will say 'frumious.'"*

However, since Carroll had the nasty habit of placing letters out of order when he created a portmanteau (neither fuming or furious begin with an "fr"), scholars are still tracking his Snarks. In our opinion, that makes it much less fun when the cleverness is lost on all of us.

We prefer J.K.R.'s style – where we at least stand a chance of getting it. One of the few early examples of a portmanteau in the Harry Potter series is the name "Gringotts," a combination of gringou (French for *miser*) and ingot (a *nugget of precious metal*). Hers are still not that easy to trace because portmanteau words are often difficult to research. You may not know where one word ends and the next begins – especially since letters are dropped, doubled, or slightly altered. In the case of Gringotts, it can look as if it is a combination of grin+got, but as goblins aren't very funny, we didn't think that was what J.K.R. intended.

Book 5 has the most elaborate use of wordplay. As always, every name has a meaning – and there are a gazillion new names in Book 5. Since there was not enough time to write up all the name information, we picked only those that are key clues. If the name was just a reinforcement of other running bits, or just clever to the plot, we will cover it in our next guide (cross fingers) – which will have full Rowlinguistics in it. We tried to include every name that gave *new* insight into the septological mysteries, but we may have missed a couple.

In the UK edition of *OoP*, Neville does a little malapropism that is a very big key to deciphering Book 5. In Chapter 16 ("The Hog's Head"), he inadvertently calls the Philosopher's Stone (that's the "Sorcerer's Stone" for U.S. readers) a ***Philological Stone***. However HP Sleuths might call it the Book 5 Rosetta Stone, since we now know that is the key to the secrets of Book 5. If you don't know the meaning of "philological," you may want to look it up. That's what you are going to be doing – if you're doing Book 5 detective work!

Are There Too Many Words in Book 5?

Book 5 is a literary wonder! Don't let the critics send you off the trail. They are just not well informed. *There are **not** too many words in Harry Potter and the Order of the Phoenix!*...That is...unless you don't care about what is going to happen in Books 6 and 7...

The people who are under the misguided impression that there are too many words in Book 5 haven't quite yet grasped the concept that this is a cerebral **Mystery**, and that the clues (unlike in a blood-and-guts thriller) are ***buried in the words!*** If HP Sleuths personally encounter any of those poor underprivileged members of society who haven't discovered the secret, you can help by opening their eyes to the *other* half of the brilliant writing that has gone into these great works of literature.

Now, you will have to be sensitive to the realization that some people will turn up their noses because they won't want to admit that they were fooled; and then there are others who will *never* get it (or even if they do, they still may not like puzzles). That is fine. One doesn't have to become a champion or even *like* chess in order to understand that it is highly complex and that it takes much more time for a Grand Master to play it, than a novice.

The important issue is that at least those who are informed will have an appreciation for why the Harry Potter books are so long. Hopefully they will also appreciate the headaches we get trying to decipher it all...!

Are There Differences Between the UK and U.S. Versions of Book 5?

Once again, we have considerable differences between the two editions. However, this time it is **not** just because they were edited for an "American" audience. It appears that the editing was done completely independently by the two publishers. Some corrections to actual errors appeared in the U.S. version but not in the UK version, and vice-versa. It seems that both publishers received the raw manuscript and edited independently. That means whole sentences are often quite different. We used one of each copy, but generally gave precedence to the UK version. Serious HP Sleuths may want to have both editions. Jim Dale's U.S. Listening Library audio version does use the Scholastic edition.

What Is Significant About the Date That Book 5 Was Released?

Harry Potter and the Order of the Phoenix was released on June 21, 2003. This date just happened to correspond to the northern Summer Solstice that year. The Summer Solstice is the date in which the sun is the highest in the sky and is the longest day of the year. The tie to a celestial date rather than a Gregorian Calendar date is significant. As with everything else in Book 5, even the release date holds clues.

(Review) How Reliable Is the Information in This Guide?

Even though this is an unauthorized Guide, all observations are based solely on what J. K. Rowling has written in her books (#1-5 and *Comic Relief* schoolbooks), what is contained on the *Bloomsbury* web site (www.bloomsbury.com), the *Scholastic* web site (www.scholastic.com), the *Warner Bros.* web site (www.harrypotter.com), and/or what has been personally stated by J.K.R. in public interviews.

Accuracy and supported evidence are highly valued by Wizarding World Press.

Please remember: We are not revealing any proprietary information as all our insights are strictly from careful literary detective work on her published works.

(Review) What Is a Septology?

There are many well-known three-volume series called "trilogies." According to J. K. Rowling, the Harry Potter stories will span a seven-volume series. As it is clearly an aggregate work (not just sequels), we are calling it a septology {"septem" = *seven* in Latin + "ology" = "logia" = *discourse* in Latin and Greek – used in words like zoology}. Before deciding on "septology," we did a search on the Internet in order to discern the best term for a seven-part series. We considered the use of "heptalogy" {"hepta = *seven* in Greek}, but there is very little precedence for its use (and it doesn't appear in the dictionary). Additionally, it is often mis-spelled — confusing it with a very nasty medical ailment. Heptalogy just doesn't work. The word "septology," however, was already in use — and commonly applied to works of science-fiction and fantasy, in particular. There are several series which have historically been described with that term. Those utilizing "sep-tology" have included very reputable reviewers from highly respected sources such as The Washington Post, ScienceFiction.com, and University professors. We thought J.K.R.'s works also deserved that recognition.

(Review) What Is an Ultimate Unofficial Mystery Guide? ...and What Is an "HP Sleuth"™ ?

THIS IS NOT A CHEAT BOOK to give away or help skip over any parts of the original stories – in fact, you will probably find yourself going back to reread in disbelief what you missed the first time! The primary objective of this Guide is to show readers how to look for the hidden clues, and then have fun speculating about what will really happen.

This is an Unofficial "Mystery Guide" (Hints Edition) to the Harry Potter stories, by Wizarding World Press. It is not authorized by J. K. Rowling, Warner Bros., Bloomsbury Publishing, or Scholastic Inc. Nonetheless, since we like what they have done for us fans, we hope that this Guide will create new excitement for Harry Potter (plus new book and merchandise sales), when everyone discovers the truly sophisticated mystery hiding in the Harry Potter stories.

The Harry Potter septology is an *epic mystery* and is considerably more intricate than it appears. This Guide specifically highlights these *mystery* aspects, including all the puzzles and brain-teasers that J. K. Rowling has painstakingly hidden within her story line. She has divulged that she purposely concealed clues along the way, and challenges us readers (we call ourselves "HP Sleuths"™) to discover them.

The goal of this Guide is to show HP Sleuths what to look for, since there are so many clever references that can slip by us (even on a third or fourth reading!). This Guide does not presume to have answers for anything that has not yet been published. Its purpose is to present reliable evidence in order to generate entertaining discussions. We encourage HP Sleuths to use this as a starting point for new theories and debates.

From the moment you uncover your first hidden clue, you will see how much fun it is being an HP Sleuth. *The second meeting of the HP Sleuth Club™ is now in session!*

> Get your official
> HP Sleuth Membership Card
> in the back of this book!

How to Read This Guide (Very Carefully) ☺
(WWP Help Desk)

Navigating This Guide

Because we are only pointing HP Sleuths to sections and not explicitly detailing our discoveries and observations, this could be frustrating (you would probably feel like going into Dumbledore's office and smashing things) if you try to read all of this as a stand-alone. The **FAQs** (Frequently Asked Questions) along with the **Running Bits (Some tricky ones)**, are completely self-explanatory, and can be read without referencing any passages. However, if you want to be able to understand *all* of the **Hints**, you will HAVE to keep your copy of *Harry Potter and the Order of the Phoenix* on hand as you read this Hints Guide.

We have pulled out our WWP Magical Toolkit and put our WWP Sleuthoscope and HP Hintoscope on the desk. Although we will be carefully watching them for signs of activity, we have asked them to try to keep still as best they can since we are trying to not make the clues too obvious yet. (Knowing those guys, that's like asking Fred and George to be serious.) Our Rememberit Quill has promised to help jog your mind when trying to think back to the first four Harry Potter Books, but it seems to be getting even more moody lately, so please forgive its peevishness.

A Hint About Hints

The Hints are divided into two types. They are *both* important because the clues are so complex and interrelated in Book 5 that you have to first recognize the smaller and less significant hints in order to understand how they direct you to the mega secrets and clues of the septology.

Items of Intrigue

This category of Hints points to clues, or is related to clues. Some are only *highly suspicious* (otherwise known as – we haven't had time to research them thoroughly), but follow the pattern of the clues we have already spotted. The rest are the indirect clues, yet are essential to understanding the big ones. These hints are generally easier to solve – typically by a quick Rememberit Quill jab of the details or careful rereading of passages from specified chapters in any of the first five Harry Potter books.

Secrets and Concealed Clues

These Hints are the biggies – guiding HP Sleuths to the heart of the secrets and clues we've discovered. These are not as easy to solve as they typically involve both rereading and external research.

We can't say for sure what JKR intended, but these are the clues that are screaming at us.

Abbreviations

Book Numbers

Throughout this Guide, to make the analysis easier (and to keep our typist sane), we will be referring to the Harry Potter books by number. Therefore, just in case, here is a cross-reference list of the books by title.

Book 1: *Harry Potter and the Philosopher's (Sorcerer's) Stone*
Book 2: *Harry Potter and the Chamber of Secrets*
Book 3: *Harry Potter and the Prisoner of Azkaban*
Book 4: *Harry Potter and the Goblet of Fire*
Book 5: *Harry Potter and the Order of the Phoenix*

J.K.R.

J. K. Rowling's name is quite short (as authors' names go); however, given the number of times we reference her name, we will use her initials (J.K.R.). We mean no disrespect with this abbreviation. We hope you understand, Ms. Rowling.

WWP

This is us. This is an abbreviation for *Wizarding World Press* – the virtual press-room where we spend real hours bringing you all these goodies.

(Review) A Clue About Clues

There are two kinds of clues that can be found in the Harry Potter books:

A story-line clue – which is specific to the book in which it is found. An example of this is that Harry's scar hurts at certain times throughout Book 1.

A septology clue – which is not resolved by the end of one book. This kind of clue relates to the whole seven-volume mystery, and will not be revealed by J.K.R. until after Book 5 (the current HP book as of the time of this writing). An example of this is Dumbledore's reluctance in Book 1 to reveal the secret behind why Voldemort wanted to kill Harry until Book 5.

NEW SPOILER WARNING!
(In case you missed the other two)

This is a Hints-only version of our "Ultimate Unofficial Guide." *New Clues* is written to allow HP Sleuths to try out their own detective skills – as we won't openly be giving everything away. Unlike our original guide, New Clues doesn't contain a summary of Book 5, and information will be discussed out of order.

As a Hints guide, this is specifically for HP Sleuths, so we are assuming that readers of *New Clues* have already read our first guide and, most of all, have finished reading Harry Potter and the Order of the Phoenix.

That means it is one big spoiler! Be forewarned. ☺

HP SLEUTH HOME PAGE

The WWP Magical Toolkit

(HP Sleuth Home Page)

Toolkit Contents

HP Sleuths have some useful tools to help them as they read. In the spirit of J.K.R.'s own humor, we have had a little fun with satire for these. Here is your box of magical mechanisms:

- **The HP Hintoscope** – This is a very delicate device that detects J.K.R.'s hints and clues about the story-line plot. When it gets near an important hint, the HP Hintoscope makes a noise to alert HP Sleuths that a hint is being detected. The more annoying it gets, the bigger the clue.

- **The WWP Sleuthoscope** – This is a super-sensitive sensor that can sniff out cleverly disguised Septology clues. It alerts using flashing and various motions. The brighter it gets and the faster it moves, the greater the Septology implications.

- **The WWP Rememberit Quill** – This is a really remarkable recording quill. It automatically transcribes all key clues and brain ticklers (Rememberits), and annoys us with rude reminders until we solve them.

- **The *Philological Stone*** – This is the Rosetta Stone to deciphering all the complex linguistics that J.K.R. has buried in Book 5. In order to help you understand and decipher all her clever linguistics, J.K.R. was kind enough to have planted a hint about how to translate Book 5. We have spent the last 3 months in a sleepless quest, searching grimy ancient archives, and have finally succeeded in laying our hands on this rare treasure. It is included it in your HP Sleuth Toolkit.

Note: Sharp HP Sleuths know that these magical devices never make random motions or sounds. By paying close attention to their reactions, you will get very precise readings that can help you pinpoint and solve the clues.

HP Sleuth Suggested Supplies
& Recommended Reading

5TH YEAR LIST

INCLUDED

- WWP Magical Toolkit
- WWP Membership & Reference Cards (Pop-outs in back of your Guide)

PREREQUISITES

✳ The Harry Potter series – including an on-hand copy of Book 5!

         Book 1 - *Harry Potter and the Philosopher's (Sorcerer's) Stone*
         Book 2 - *Harry Potter and the Chamber of Secrets*
         Book 3 - *Harry Potter and the Prisoner of Azkaban*
         Book 4 - *Harry Potter and the Goblet of Fire*
         Book 5 - *Harry Potter and the Order of the Phoenix*

HIGHLY RECOMMENDED

✳ Textbook: *Fantastic Beasts and Where to Find Them,* by Newt Scamander

✳ Background Reading: *Quidditch Through the Ages,* by Kennilworthy Whisp

✳ HP Sleuth detective quill and parchment -12 rolls (or an official Harry Potter notebook)

SUGGESTED READING AND OTHER MEDIA

Reference

✳ *Dictionary of Phrase and Fable* (Brewer's or Oxford versions)

✳ *Bartleby's Reference* (Printed or Online)

✳ Dictionary – Hermione's favorite tools - the biggest (and heaviest) English-language dictionary (preferably International) that you can find, and a local reference library.

Literature & Art

☾ Aeschylus - *Prometheus Bound*

☾ L. Frank Baum – *The Land of Oz*

☾ Lewis Carroll, – *Alice in Wonderland,* (we use annotated edition by Donald J. Gray – Norton) (Mad Hatter Tea Party), *Through the Looking Glass,* "Hunting of the Snark," Discussion of "Raven-to-Writing Desk" (http://www.straightdope.com/classics/a5_266.html)

☾ Emily Dickinson – "I'm Nobody"

☾ E.R. Eddison – *The Worm Ouroboros*

☾ T.S. Eliot – *Murder in the Cathedral,* "Burnt Norton"

- Homer – *The Odyssey*
- Washington Irving – "Legend of Sleepy Hollow," "Rip Van Winkle"
- W.W. Jacobs – "The Monkey's Paw"
- James Joyce – (In moderation!), *Finnegan's Wake, Portrait of the Artist as a Young Man*
- Franz Kafka – *Penal Colony, Metamorphosis, The Trial*
- Rudyard Kipling – *Rikki-Tikki-Tavi*
- Leonardo da Vinci – sketch "Vitruvian Man"
- Michelangelo – painting "Crucifixion of Peter" (hint – upside-down)
- John Milton – *Paradise Lost*
- A.A. Milne – *House at Pooh Corner*
- George Orwell – *1984, Animal Farm*
- Charles Perrault – *Contes du Temps*
- Edgar Allan Poe – "The Raven"
- Philip Pullman – *His Dark Materials* (theologically controversial)
- Saki – "The Open Window"
- Jean Paul Sartre – *Huis Clos (No Exit)*
- William Shakespeare – "King Henry V," (Act III, Scene 6), "Romeo and Juliet," "Macbeth"
- Robert Louis Stevenson – *Treasure Island*
- Frank R. Stockton – "The Lady or the Tiger"
- Alfred Lord Tennyson – "Sir Galahad"
- J.R.R. Tolkien – All Works
- Mark Twain (Samuel Clemens) – *Puddin' head Wilson*
- H.G. Wells – "The Red Room," "Under the Knife"

Classical Mythology/Mysticism Resources

- Greek, Roman, Norse, Egyptian Mythology
- Druid Legends & Monuments
- Ouroboros Eastern Mysticism resource

Kids Korner Nursery Rhymes

- ☾ *The House that Jack Built*
- ☾ *Humpty Dumpty*
- ☾ *Jack and Jill*
- ☾ *Little Jack Horner*
- ☾ *Peter Piper*
- ☾ *Sing a Song of Sixpence*
- ☾ *Three Blind Mice*

Movies/TV

- ☾ *Forbidden Planet*, Metro-Goldwyn-Mayer
- ☾ *The Highlander,* Fox/EMI Films
- ☾ Monty Python - *Life of Brian,* Warner Bros./Orion Pictures
- ☾ *Rosencrantz and Guildenstern are Dead,* Cinecom International
- ☾ *Time of Their Lives* -Abbott and Costello, Universal Studios
- ☾ *Young Frankenstein* - Mel Brooks, Fox
- ☾ *Dr. Who* TV series
- ☾ *Star Trek* TV series
- ☾ *Deathtrap* (Michael Caine, Christopher Reeve – can be controversial!), Warner Bros.

Music Lyrics

- ☾ Moody Blues – "The Dream" from *Threshold of a Dream*
- ☾ Gilbert & Sullivan – *The Mikado*
- ☾ Caravan – *In the Land of Grey and Pink* - Album

TCG

- ☾ The Harry Potter TCG (Trading Card Game) by Wizards of the Coast (www.wizards.com).

Secrets of the HP Super Sleuth

NEW COROLLARY ADDED

The clues in Book 5 are brilliant!

Just as J.K.R. intended, OoP had us "running in circles." With proper-sized thesaurus and some dictionaries, it is not impossible (with a few sleepless weeks) to cross-reference the wordplay in order to identify keywords and running bits. However, what took almost all of our time was sorting them out so we could see the patterns and understand the clues.

In Books 1-4, a running bit in the form of a "flute" or "sing-song voice," could point us to a "music" hint. That would usually have been the keyword clue.

However, in Book 5, J.K.R. has purposely used *ambiguous* keywords as running bits!

A seemingly simple phrase like "Elephant and Castle" may be pointing us to "sharp" hints or "trunk" hints. But then... would that be a "trunk" like a *nose*, or like a *chest* of clothes? ...Or could that be a trunk of a *tree*? There are *noses*, *chests* (*on the body*), and *trees* – all proliferating throughout Book 5, it is impossible to know which one she meant without a year of research (or some legilimens skills).

Our new corollary to Rule #1, *Juxtaposition [jux-ta-position]*, can help. By scouting the area in which the words are used, it is possible to spot additional hints that give the true intent of the clue. Then again, in the "trunk" example, even if we found out it related to noses, we would have yet another problem because both *smells* and *injured noses* are running bit clues as well. (groan) You get the idea.

*We will give you one hint that would have helped us had we known from the beginning: as mind boggling as it may seem – when in doubt, assume **all** are clues.*

Book 5 is one huge cerebral cortex charmer! (That's "brain-teaser" for those who have misplaced their *Philological Stone*.) Every time we cracked the code and stripped away a layer, we found another one laying in wait. It is unbelievable that J.K.R. could have done this at all – let alone in less than three years. ...And you thought Book 5 was about stealing an orb?

If you have a Ph.D. in language and literature, you would say Book 5 is a literary dream, but for the philologically challenged, it can be a nightmare. J.K.R. gives us clues by playing with words in a manner similar to that utilized by Lewis Carroll (*Alice in Wonderland*) – but in a much more subtle way – so you don't always realize she is doing it (see Rowlinguistics FAQ).

We have made your task tons easier by pointing you directly to the running bits and segments containing the clues. Now all you have to do is spot the exact clue, based on the hints we are giving, fit the pieces together, and solve the mysteries. Well...it's easier said than done because it's going to take some brainwork. However, we know that's what HP Sleuths crave, so we are sure you will have a jolly good time picking out these gems.

WWPs' Rules of Constant Vigilance

We have uncovered the "secret" to being an HP Super Sleuth. If you want to consider yourself a good HP Sleuth, there are 4 rules to keep in mind about the way J.K. Rowling writes:

Rule #1

IF SHE REINFORCES IT, SHE MEANS IT – HP Sleuths need to focus on these kind of clues. Like everyone else, J.K.R. is not flawless, and she has made a few minor errors in her books. Unfortunately, a few people may try to put special meaning on those or use those to debunk her intentional, masterful clues. The general rule here is to ignore conflicting information or a one-time questionable reference. However, if she repeats a reference/clue (no matter how subtle), she means for us to take it seriously. We do.

> **Corollary**
> **1a) Juxtaposition [Jux-ta-position] of repeated information (especially running bits) points to clues.**

Rule #2

IF SHE SUDDENLY INTERRUPTS SOMETHING (AND NEVER FINISHES), SHE'S HIDING A KEY CLUE! – What was that? If Harry misses a lesson, if a character gets cut off while saying something, or even if someone forgets to ask a question, it's probably because we are being tormented by J.K.R.. HP Sleuths should take note that if we know that we missed out on something, it is almost as good as knowing the information itself – especially if you like mysteries.

Rule #3

THERE'S NO SUCH THING AS A COINCIDENCE - When a character conveniently shows up at the right time (or wrong time), or when the same topic keeps mysteriously popping up over and over, it is a clue begging for attention. In her magical world, J.K.R. has put a high emphasis on fate, plus there is often a good reason why things that look like coincidences happen. Yet, she also has a mischievous sense of humor, so HP Sleuths have to work hard to also avoid the red herrings. Often, her red herrings are just incomplete clues, so that if we pick up on all the "real" clues, we find that she has actually given us enough information to sort it out accurately.

Rule #4

DON'T TAKE A CHARACTER'S WORD FOR IT - Characters often interpret events for us in her books. That is what characters are supposed to do. However, their analysis will be colored by their own personality and their particular perspective of the events. Just because the character has an explanation does not mean it is correct. J.K.R. constantly uses this technique to throw us off the trail, and a good HP Sleuth must be wary of that trick.

> **Corollaries**
> **4a) Hermione is usually right (except when she gets emotional).**
> **4b) Ron is usually wrong (except when he makes a joke about it).**

CONSTANT VIGILANCE! ☺

The Pocket Version

WWP's Rules of Constant Vigilance!

Never let your guard down with J.K.R. These are the Rules to remember(unless your memory is as bad as Gilderoy's). Rules for HP Sleuths:

1) **If she reinforces it, she means it (and wants us to remember it).**
     1a) Juxtaposition counts!
2) **If she suddenly interrupts something (never finishes), she's hiding a key clue!**
3) **There's no such thing as a coincidence.**
4) **Don't take a character's word for it.**
     4a) Hermione is usually right (except when she gets emotional).
     4b) Ron is usually wrong (except when he makes a joke about it).

(see WWP Help Desk FAQs for full explanation)

BOOK 5 CLUES

Old Bits and New Bits

New Characters in Book 5

This is a list of characters who are new to Book 5 ...or who had been mentioned previously but only now are becoming important to the mystery. Many of them hold clues, so you should have them on your mind as you sleuth Book 5. We think we got everyone – five people worked on this. Just please don't hit if we missed anyone....

NEW (OR NEWLY IMPORTANT) CHARACTERS IN BOOK 5

Students

(CHARACTERS)	(BIT PLAYERS)	(OFFSTAGE)
Hannah Abbott	Euan Abercrombie	Bole
Susan Bones	Miles Bletchley	Bradley
Michael Corner	Terry Boot	Chambers
Marietta Edgecombe	Eddie Carmichael	Derrick
Anthony Goldstein	Roger Davies	Vicky Frobisher
Luna Lovegood	Harold Dingle	Daphne Greengrass
Montague	Andrew Kirke	Geoffrey Hooper
Zacharias Smith	Theodore Nott	Stebbins (Pensieve)
	Adrian Pucey	Patricia Stimpson
	Jack Sloper	Summerby
	Warrington	Kenneth Towler
		Rose Zeller

Relatives

(CHARACTERS)	(BIT PLAYERS)	(OFFSTAGE)
Amelia Susan Bones	Alphard Black	Elladora Black
Bellatrix Black Lestrange	Regulus Black	Edgar Bones
Rastaban Lestrange	Aberforth Dumbledore (?)	Andromeda Black Tonks
Rodolphus Lestrange	Madam Edgecombe	Ted Tonks
Alice Longbottom	Narcissa Black Malfoy	Cassandra Trelawney
Frank Longbottom	Montague's parents	
Mrs. Longbottom (Gran)		

Teachers

(CHARACTERS)
Dolores Jane Umbridge

Other Humans

(CHARACTERS)	(BIT PLAYERS)	(OFFSTAGE)
Avery	Agnes	Millicent Bagnold
Broderick Bode	Bob	Baruffio
Dedalus Diggle	Dawlish	Stubby Boardman
Elphias Doge	Eric Munch	Pierre Bonaccord
Antonin Dolohov	Jugson	Caradoc Dearborn
Arabella Figg	Gordon	Mark Evans
Mundungus Fletcher	Hog's Head barman (?)	Mary Dorkins
Hestia Jones	"Dangerous" Dai Llewellen	Benjy Fenwick
Griselda Marchbanks	Malcolm	Gladys Gudgeon
Alastor Moody	Madam Marsh	Warty Harris
Perkins	Mulciber	Marlene McKinnon
Sturgis Podmore	Mr. Prentice	Dorcas Meadowes
Augustus Rookwood	Madam Puddifoot	Araminta Meliflua
Kingsley Shacklebolt	Augustus Pye	Mrs. Number Seven
Professor Tofty	Hippocrates Smethwyck	Tiberius Ogden
Nymphadora Tonks	Miriam Strout	Fabian Prewett
Emmeline Vance	Janus Thickey	Gideon Prewett
	Willy Widdershins (Will?)	Doris Purkiss
	Williamson	Barry Ryan
		Scrimgeour
		Ladislaw Zamojski

Creatures and Entities

(CHARACTERS)	(BIT PLAYERS)	(OFFSTAGE)
Mrs. Black	Animate armor	Bungy the budgie
Dilys Derwent	Barnabas the Barmy	Elfrida Cragg
Armando Dippet	Fortescue	Lachlan the Lanky
Everard	Staff room Gargoyles	Paracelsus
Grawp	Latin-mumbling statue	Urquhart Rackharrow
Golgomath	Magorian	Ragnok
Karkus	Snow-white centaur	Wilfred the Wistful
Kreacher	Tenebrus	
Phineas Nigellus	Mr. Tibbles	

Updates to Books 1-4 Analyses

It doesn't take magic to become enchanted by the Harry Potter books. You can read them several times and still have fun without even thinking about the underlying mysteries. Once you start picking up on the clues, however, you can't help but be spellbound by the magic in the words. And for some reason, you never stop finding clues....

We at WWP keep thinking that J.K.R. cannot possibly have crammed anything more into those books – that we have already picked them to the bone. Ha! Yes, we are *still* discovering new treasures hidden in the first four books, and also finding out that we missed a few theories and potential clues that might come in handy for solving the mysteries in Book 5.

Here are the most important ones for sleuthing Book 5, which didn't make it into our previous Guide.

Neville's Gran and Uncle Algie

Have you noticed that the more important the character, the less we know about their background? (sigh) We now have confirmation from Book 5 that Neville is a key character (even if Voldemort doesn't think so). Yet, what do we know about his Gran and the rest of his family? Other than Gran being the vulture lady and Uncle Algie being the guy who dropped Neville out of a window (friendly types) – nothing much. Are we convinced that Gran and Uncle Algie are "good guys"? Could Uncle Algie be making sure Neville doesn't recover? What happens during Neville's visits to St Mungo's? Could someone be administering any "booster" charms? You gotta wonder...

Neville's Toad Trevor

What's going on with Trevor? Could he be around to watch out for Neville, or maybe to spy on him? If so, then why is Trevor always running off - does that make sense? Is that because Neville's own mind is so unfocused, or is something/someone prodding Trevor to take off? As we had mentioned on our site, we had not really thought about some Trevor clues until too late – our first Guide had already been printed. If you recall, Trevor has been awfully eager to escape from Neville's grip every chance he gets, and was found lurking in the bathroom at the end of Book 1. We are sure that it was a general hint about a certain bathroom in Book 2, but we also agree with the opinion that Hagrid's hen house is a bit too close to Trevor for comfort (if you're not sure what we're getting at, look in the "Bs" in your copy of *Fantastic Beasts and Where to Find Them*). He does seem to be a toad on a mission.

Lily's Parents

In our first Guide, we questioned if Lily's parents (the Evans) might have been wizards hiding out as Muggles. We also thought it was possible that one or both of her parents could have been Squibs. However, we hadn't realized that we never actually came out and said that in the Guide until HP Sleuths started asking why we didn't think they could be Squibs. But we do! We need to alert all HP Sleuths that is a possibility. We also questioned whether Lily or Petunia could have been adopted. Based on new information from Headmaster Dumbledore, we are now sure that if Lily were adopted, Petunia would have to be too – as they have been confirmed to be blood sisters. Dumbledore specified that the charm protecting Harry had to come down through his mother's blood relative, and that Petunia was the only remaining blood relative on his mother's side. If one or both of Lily's parents were Squibs, that would explain:

* why the Evans were so proud to have a witch in the family
* why Lily's parents allowed her to practice magic at home
* why Petunia was so resentful (if she knew)

Snape

There are three kinds of HP Sleuths – those who believe that Snape is a vampire, those who don't believe Snape is a vampire, and those who....

We have a revised opinion about Snape. This is what we have posted about the issues surrounding the "Is Snape a vamp?" controversy:

Daylight
Not a Vamp – In most accounts, vamps can't go out into the sun (it can be lethal!), but Snape does.
Vamp – If Snape can do a complex potion that renders a werewolf safe, why couldn't he do a potion that would allow a vampire to be exposed to sunlight for short time (sunblock potion SPF 5000)? He is greasy enough....

Food
Not a Vamp – Because they are "undead," vampires don't need regular food - only blood, but Snape eats food at the table during the feasts.
Vamp – Just because Snape appears to "eat" at the table, doesn't mean he actually eats human food. He may have a special "diet" sent up to his plate by the house-elves. Remember - Honeydukes carries blood-flavored treats!

Reflection
Not a Vamp – Vamps are famous for not having a reflection from a mirror, but Snape was reflected in the "Foe Glass."
Vamp – The Foe Glass has very special magical properties, and considering that Harry saw Snape's "reflection" before Snape had even entered the room, indicates that the "foe" is not really being "reflected," but is a magical image. Nonetheless, it was *emphasized* that Snape took a look.

<u>Sleepless</u>
Not a Vamp – Vamps only repose (not a true sleep) during the day and are up all night, but Snape has been seen at night in a nightshirt.

Vamp – Although we have seen Snape in a night shirt, we have also seen that he is always awake (and often wandering around) whenever Harry is getting into trouble at night. Maybe Snape has "night clothes" just to give himself a clean (not-so-greasy), comfortable change of clothes while he is up at night?

<u>Definition</u>
Not a Vamp – *Goblet of Fire,* Chapter 10, Percy's comments on the stamping out of vampires: *"...Guidelines for the Treatment of Non-Wizard Part-Humans—"* (aka vampires). If a vamp is a "non-wizard," then Snape *can't* be a vamp (right?).

Vamp – Uhhh...uh... we have been re-thinking this vamp thing... yet we're thinking about all those *other* clues... let's see...ummm... Wait!

What if he were ***part vampire?*** 😊

So... Is Snape a vampire or isn't he? Maybe the answer is "Yes."

Book 4 Anomaly *(Translation – Potential Clue)*

There was one *huge* difference between the UK and the U.S. versions of *Book 4* that we didn't see until our first Guide had printed. It reminds us of the kind of editing discrepancies we have found with Book 5. The trouble is, the one in Book 4 dramatically impacts sleuthing, and we aren't sure if it was intentional or not. (We are told that, oddly, the U.S. and Canadian versions match, though we haven't seen one to verify). So far, we haven't heard of it being changed, and we were tracking it all the way until July of 2003.

On pages 10 and 12 of the U.S. editions Voldemort and Wormtail use the word "murder" when talking about their plans. On pages 15 and 16 of the UK version, they use the word "curse." If the correct word is "murdered," who else was murdered? Here are the variations (plus Priori order):

EDITIONS WITH DEATH/MURDER (JAMES 1st)
Scholastic - *HC* - 1st ed., 1st printing

EDITIONS WITH OBSTACLE/CURSE (JAMES 1st)
Bloomsbury/UK - *HC* - 1st ed., 1st printing
Bloomsbury/UK - *HC* - Deluxe - 1st ed., 1st printing

EDITIONS WITH DEATH/MURDER (LILY 1st)
Scholastic - *HC* - ed: 23   0/0 01 02 03 04
Scholastic - *Paper* - ed: 12 11 10 9 8 7 6 5 4 3 2 1   2 3 4 5 7/0   40

EDITIONS WITH OBSTACLE/CURSE (LILY 1st)
Bloomsbury/UK - *HC* - ed: 20
Bloomsbury/UK - *Paper* - 1st ed., 1st printing

Bits and Rememberits

Rememberits

RUNNING BITS

It's not a matter of finding the running bits – it's more like – can we keep from falling over them! There are so many that we could write a whole guide just on the running bits in Book 5. Hope you have your thesaurus "adroitly accessible." (hehe) This is not a simple repetition of words like in the previous books (eg. lots of "eye" and "nose" references). J.K.R. has gotten extremely sneaky. She has *disguised* the running bits this time, using synonyms, puns, literary references, and even code-like messages. When you begin to realize what she has done, you start to really appreciate J.K.R.'s wizardry.

But then reality sinks in. While those are a lot of fun, they make the job of an HP Sleuth almost impossible (couldn't be what she had in mind, could it?). The red herrings are no longer simple plot decoys, but either a big clue or a big fish... or even both! There are often several hints for every running bit in Book 5, so it is difficult to know which meaning (if any) J.K.R. intended. Her extensive use of homonyms in Book 5 doesn't make it any easier either.

Here's an example:

One of the most prominent running bits is **"bark"** or **"barking."** That can be interpreted as the *bark of a dog*. Since we now know that it is Padfoot who died, that seems to imply that the running bit was there to point us to Sirius. However, "bark" can also mean the bark of a tree. Since the word "trunk" is also a running bit, should we associate "bark" with *tree* as well? Just to complicate things, "barking" can also be used the way Uncle Vernon likes to use it – to mean *barking mad*. We know that "mad" is not only another running bit, but is assuredly Harry's biggest emotion throughout Book 5, and defines the way Luna described herself ("as insane as I am"). So, what meaning do we attribute to this hairy running bit? (sigh) That's where jux-ta-position will help you.

You are starting to get the picture. And take our word for it – this was one of the *easy* ones!

What we will do to help, is to tell you what the running bits are. Not only will you have fun spotting them, but there are so many (we have found *over ten* in one sentence), that they are generally easy to find. Here is an extreme example from Chapter 28 ("Snape's Worst Memory") to show how prolific the bits are in Book 5:

*"Dragons comprised entirely of green and gold sparks were **soaring** up and down the **corridors**, emitting **loud** fiery blasts and bangs as they went; shock-ing-**pink** Catherine **wheels five feet in diameter** were whizzing lethally through the air like so many flying **saucers**; rockets with long **tails** of brilliant **silver** stars were ricocheting off the walls; sparklers were writing **swear words [toilet-related]** in **midair** of their **own accord...**"*

Because there are so many of them in each chapter, we will handle it the way we did in our original Guide – which is to give some examples and then let you HP Sleuths spot the rest on your own. The examples that we give may not nec-essarily be the most important instances in which they are used. If they are of more significance than just being there to taunt us, we will include it in our Hints section. The purpose of the "tricky" Running Bits we use in each chapter is to show some of the clever (we're being kind – the word should be "devious") ways J.K.R. has disguised the running bits so we don't notice them right away; or to show how she has packed multiple running bits into one phrase. By observing those, you will be able to acquire the technique as well as an appreci-ation for the "subtle science and exact art" of hunting running bits (thank you, Professor Snape).

One thing that HP Sleuths should practice is "mixing and matching" of running bits. As we explained in the Help Desk section at the front of this Guide, the run-ning bits and clues are all puns with multiple meanings. "A trunk" can be a nose, a chest, or a tree. So, you need to look at the running bits and attempt mixing and matching them up to see all the possible combinations. For example, start with the running bit "spindly." Think about other forms of the word – the obvious is spindle. A spindle can mean a spike – and there are "sharp" and "poking" run-ning bits, so you know that is an important meaning for it. A spindle can also be a spinning wheel/weaving tool. "Wheels" and "spidery" are both running bits as well. Now try matching legs and spindly with chairs from your Running Bits list. There are oodles of chairs and tables with spindly legs in Book 5. And those are only a few combinations for that example. By seeing the different combinations J.K.R. has used, you can start recognizing the clues in order to solve the mysteries.

Please keep in mind that we have only pointed out some of the more subtle run-ning bits in each chapter. The pages are pecked with them. Use your Running Bits reference card from the back of this book and have a bit of fun finding them!

—————— *Book 5 Running Bits* ——————

2s, 4s, 5s, 10s, 12s
　9 of 10, 14s
Across, Crossing
Automatic (actions)
Babies, Calves,
　Babytalk
Balance, Measure
Bark, Barking
Bells, Rings,
　Tones
Bolts, Padlocks,
　Chains
Brains, Minds
Bubbles, Balloons,
Ceiling
Chairs
Circles, Round,
　Wheels
Color (pink, blue,
　orange, silver)
Cracking

Crosses
Doors, Corridors
Dreaming
Ducking
Ears (hurt)
Eggs
Eyes (bulging,
　　black, hurt)
Frogs, Toads
Glass
Grims
Growing, Swelling
Hands, Claws (hurt)
Hats & Socks, Wool
Heads (severed,
　　Missing)
Hearts
Hems & Skirts
Horns
Hot/Cold,
　　Flame/Freezing

Jumping/Falling
　Back
Kings, Rooks, Crowns
Knees
Legs/Feet (many)
Levitating, Midair,
　Soar
Mad, Nuts
March
Moon, Planets (Luna,
　Phases, Umbra)
Mouse, Mice
Mouths (open)
Muttering, Mumbling
Necks
Noises, Screeching
Noses (hurt)
Pairs, Doubles, Mate
Pies
Pipes
Pounding, Hammer

Regurgitating
Rubbish
Sharp, Edge, Poking
Silence, Muffle
Sliding, Sinking
Spindly, Spidery
Spots, Dots, Ink
Stinking, Smells
Stone
Stubby, Stump
Tableware
Tails, Queues
Toilets, Dung
Towers
Trunk, Chest, Tree
Turns (left, right)
Twisted, Coiling
Upside-down
Vanishing
Water, Rain, Mist

Please note: *In order to print your pop-outs, we had to rush the list out early. So, Reference Cards are missing: Balance/Measure, Ceiling, Claws, Horns, Glass, Planets, Rubbish, and Noises/Screeching, plus "Hems & Skirts" is out of order.*

—————— *Interesting Tidbits* ——————

MISSING PERSONS LIST

Totally Missing
　　Aragog
　　Ludovic Bagman
　　Bloody Baron
　　Crouches Jr/Sr (the bodies)
　　Karkaroff
　　Myrtle
　　Wormtail / Peter Pettigrew

Suspiciously Absent
　　Fleur
　　Krum
　　Nagini (?)
　　Winky

Let's Go Snark Hunting...

————— * —————

Chapter 1 Clues

(DUDLEY DEMENTED)

FAQs

ON WHAT DATE DOES BOOK 5 BEGIN?

On what day does *any* Harry Potter book begin? Ask a fan and they will most likely immediately inform you that the books begin on Harry's birthday. But that's the kind of answer that makes our anally-retentive Rememberit Quill ooze ink! Yes, Book 1 technically began just after Halloween. On the other hand, the reason we don't consider that book to "begin" then is that the first chapter is treated as background information. The events throughout the rest of the series are generally viewed from *Harry's perspective*, but in Chapter 1 of Book 1, Harry's perspective was a bit (shall we say) *small*.

Now, Book 5 has also deviated from the pattern slightly (which makes the WWP Sleuthoscope slightly restless). To set the record straight, according to the official court records at Harry's hearing {Chapter 8, "The Hearing"}, the events that kick-started Book 5 occurred on August second (two days after Harry's birthday).

WHAT ARE THE MYSTERIES BEHIND WANDLESS MAGIC?

Wandless magic in J.K.R.'s world seems to work very similarly to the way extrasensory perception (ESP) is described in our own world. With ESP, the most frequent accounts of people having reportedly moved objects (telekinesis) are when they are very afraid or angry. Similarly, the most frequent ESP reports of psychic communication (telepathy) are when a close companion (human or otherwise) is badly injured or has passed on. In other words, extremely strong emotions supposedly trigger extrasensory events that would normally not be possible. We see that in wizards; emotions can tap latent power. That is what happens to child wizards when they get upset and the magic just sorta slips out. That is what happened to Harry with the "Vanishing Glass" and all his other unintentional uses of magic. Aunt Marge and her dog, Ripper, can be considered a real inspiration for inducing magic. 😊

At the end of Book 4, when Dumbledore got very angry about Imposter Moody, the description was that he "radiated" power. We also know from Harry's attempt to zap Bellatrix with the Cruciatus Curse at the end of Book 5, that a wizard's mental state has a *lot* to do with performing magic. If Dumbledore, or any wizard, can "radiate" power at times, can a wizard purposely focus external power?

In Chapter 2 {"A Peck of Owls"} from Book 5, we saw Harry's wand unintentionally send out sparks when he was infuriated with Uncle Vernon. We have even seen Harry perform *wanded* magic when his wand wasn't even in his hand! Then there was Moody's painfully graphic description in Chapter 3 {"The Advance Guard"} of accidents that can happen by stashing your wand in your back pocket (that guy is a bit morbid). So, Harry isn't the only one who can do that. In our original Guide, we contemplated what Ollivander was implying when he said that you wouldn't get as good results from someone else's wand. If "the wand chooses the wizard," would that not imply a special relationship between a wizard and his wand?

What proportion of the wizarding community can intentionally do wandless magic? That ability does not seem to be common, and yet certain magic appears to require it. For instance, Animagi transformations must be wandless magic as Sirius changed frequently at Azkaban, and yet they should have taken his wand away (plus, we don't recall seeing Snuffles use a wand to change back). We also have some indication it's not very common from what happened with Severus in Chapter 28 {"Snape's Worst Memory"}. Even if just a few wizards are capable of doing wandless magic, what are the ramifications of the mere existence of that ability? If you are interested in knowing more details about what could happen under those circumstances, it was the main theme in a classic science-fiction movie called *Forbidden Planet*.

Based on what we have seen of powerful wizards, we are probably to assume that strong emotions are quite useful – meaning the wizard can focus their emotions directly into their magic. Harry seems to have a lot of emotion lately, doesn't he?

What Causes Harry's Scar to Hurt?

Using the evidence we have so far, apparently the only person who can cause Harry's scar to hurt is Voldemort. Before Book 5, we can verify that Voldemort was present (or in a rage) whenever Harry's scar alerted. When Harry's scar hurt around Quirrell, Voldemort was there. When it hurt during the "dreams" he had in Book 4, he had been paying Voldemort a little house call. Even when it hurt around Crouch, we know that Voldemort was throwing a fit back at the cemetery because Harry had just slipped through his fingers (yet again*) and was returning to bear witness of Voldy's rebirthing to Dumbledore. Now, in Book 5, every incident of Harry's scar pains, where we could *verify* the cause, was due to... Lord Voldything. (When we discuss Chapter 13, we give a hint as to what triggered that indistinct pain.)

Harry has encountered Death Eaters and former Death Eaters throughout the septology. We have no evidence that Lucius Malfoy, Wormtail, Karkaroff, Snape, or even a crowd of 10 Death Eaters in the Department of Mysteries, can so much as make his scar twinge. Yet, Voldemort only needs to feel a bit giddy lately, and Harry gets a big headache. And the more intense Voldemort's emotion, the worse it hurts.

The implications of this are that we either need to pay very careful attention to what Voldything has been up to at all times, or we had better worry whether anyone else can set off Harry's scar alarm. Right now, based on what we know, we're not in a worrying frame of mind. So, until we see further evidence, we will assume that a painful scar means Voldemort is the culprit.

—————— *Running Bits* (some tricky ones) ——————

WHEELS (YOU MIGHT ALSO WANT TO NOTE THE SOUND)
"*A soft ticking noise came from several expensive racing* **bikes that they were wheeling along.**"

CIRCLES, ROUND, CORNER
"*...asking him* round *for tea...*"
"*She had* **rounded** *the* **corner**..."
"*thoughts* **whirled around**"

———————— *Hints* ————————

✳ *Items of Intrigue* ✳

MUGGLE NEWS Harry didn't hear anything important on the local Muggle news. Should HP Sleuths question that? For example, before the summer of 2003, we would have said that a major drought in England seems a bit suspicious; however, given the uncanny way that J.K.R.'s series has paralleled our Muggle world, we'll just leave it up to HP Sleuths to contemplate. If you recall, in Chapter 30 {"The Pensieve"} of Book 4, Dumbledore (who monitors the Muggle news) recognized important news that, to be Frank, was probably barely more than an obituary. So now, think about Chapter 9 {"The Midnight Duel"} in Book 1 – Draco did say something about having a near-miss on a broomstick. And in Book 5, Hermione did point out to Harry that he missed quite a few things in the *Daily Prophet*...

HARRY'S THOUGHTS Notice (hint, hint) how Harry's thoughts seemed to drift a bit *beyond his mind* as he lies there in the bushes thinking about his aunt and uncle.

POLKISS AND PIERS Now, this should be a no-brainer for the more dedicated HP Sleuths – unfortunately, easy ones like this are a rare breed. Where have we seen the names *Polkiss* and *Piers* before? Our rude Rememberit Quill is busy scribbling... 🖋 *If you can't remember this character from Book 1, you'd better take Remedial Harry Potter before reading on.* ✒

DOBBY'S POWERS Harry mentioned Dobby's powers in this chapter. Do you agree with Harry's opinion concerning Dobby's capabilities? (Hint -- you should.)

THE DARKNESS The darkness caused by the Dementors is, according to Harry, deathly real and very powerful magic. Harry's observations of their "sphere of influence" are making both the HP Hintoscope and WWP Sleuthoscope shiver.

BIRTHDAY GOODIES Doesn't Harry usually get a cake for his birthday? At least he got something chocolate. We're getting a taste of Rule #3.

DÉJÀ VU The way Book 5 begins has a bit of a déjà vu feel to it. Plus, it somehow flows with the way the book ends. HP Sleuths who are of the more daring type when it comes to literature may want to take a short cruise through *Finnegan's Wake,* by James Joyce. (Note: we wouldn't pretend to imply that anyone should attempt to read it all the way through – unless you happen to be a Buckley-style linguist.) Another work you may find reminiscent of the theme of the beginning of Book 5 is *Paradise Lost,* by John Milton.

✳ *Secrets and Concealed Clues* ✳

RADIATING POWER Harry was definitely in a highly emotional state here. By observing the incident between Uncle Vernon and Harry, what can we conclude about Harry's ability to "radiate" power as described in the FAQs above?

THE 10-YEAR-OLD J.K.R. really does have Dumbledore's sense of humor. She zapped us here. On her website (www.jkrowling.co.uk), she revealed that Mark Evans is a "nobody" (poor guy). You still may want to mark down his first name for further inspection, but he has no relationship to Lily. See what other HP Sleuths have said about him: www.newclues.mugglenet.com.

HARRY'S TAUNTING When Harry provoked Dudley, the description of his taunting is a bit suspicious. Based on what we now know of Harry's mind, it may be a good idea to reread that passage.

MAGICAL FEELINGS The sounds that accompany magic are being reinforced. However, what interests us most is that as Harry walked along, he contemplated that he was convinced something magical was going on. This feeling could be similar to the movie/series "The Highlander," if you want to research it some more.

CLUES ALL AROUND The Dementors are still going after Harry (remember his near-Kiss in Book 3?). If you read carefully, you can discover a bit more about what Dementors are (or, that is, what they are not – as those creatures seem to be missing something). *Most importantly,* HP Sleuths should review their copy of *Fantastic Beasts and Where to Find Them* (Highly Recommended for 5th-Years) to compare this attack with that of another dark, very deadly creature, on which a Patronus Charm is the only defense. Several key clues seem to be embedded in there – including one that may bring into question an event from Chapter 15 {"The Forbidden Forest"} in Book 1.

Chapter 2 Clues

(A PECK OF OWLS)

FAQs

HOW DOES OWL POST WORK?

For being so intelligent, how is it that the owls smash into windows? The answer may also hold a key to owl delivery magic. Consider what might have caused the owl to head for a closed window.

We still may not understand owl delivery, however, in Book 5 we have a whole flock of new evidence about how it works. Notice the recipient's address can be verbal, written, or even in code (such as in Chapter 14 {"Percy and Padfoot"}), or that additional instructions can be given *verbally*. (Ron's fingers sure seemed to have noticed in Chapter 4 {"Number Twelve Grimmauld Place"}). The most intriguing insight comes again from Chapter 14, where Harry feels it necessary to *whisper* his instructions to Hedwig while in the Owlery. So, whoooooo would have overheard Harry?

WHAT DID AUNT PETUNIA'S HOWLER MEAN BY "REMEMBER MY LAST"?

We know from Chapter 37 {"The Lost Prophecy"} in Book 5, that it was Dumbledore, himself, who sent the Howler. Why didn't Harry recognize his voice? Would Dumbledore have needed to disguise his voice?

Even though the part about Dumbledore's "last" message was a bit cryptic to us readers, Aunt Petunia seemed to know very well what it meant. What communication would that have been? It could have been the letter he left with the baby Harry on their doorstep, which explained their commitment on taking in Harry. But it may not have been. Just to be sure, HP Sleuths may want to investigate exactly when it was that Aunt Petunia and Dumbledore would have "last" communicated. (Hint -- there does appear to be some contact with the Dursleys – for instance in Chapter 5 {"The Whomping Willow"} from Book 2.)

HOW DOES HARRY'S PROTECTION AT PRIVET DRIVE WORK?

According to Voldemort in Chapter 33 {"The Death Eater"} of Book 4, due to the ancient magic that Dumbledore has cast, he can't touch Harry at the house on Privet Drive. Dumbledore's description of this magic in Chapter 37 {"The Lost Prophecy"} tells us that the protection is based on a mother's love. Since love is something that is repulsive to Lord Voldything, he will not learn that magic, and therefore has trouble combating it. Harry is safe at Privet Drive.

Yet, there are still several questions about how that safety works. How did Dobby get in? Does it extend beyond the bounds of the property? We had thought it did until we saw the Dementor attack just a few blocks away. Dumbledore said that Harry only needs to visit Privet Drive to have the protection all year long. What *kind* of protection? Could it be that Harry is vulnerable to anyone *except* Voldemort?

Dumbledore's words in Chapter 37 {"The Lost Prophecy"}, were that the original letter that accompanied baby Harry was left on "her" doorstep. This may have been a convenient way of phrasing it, but if you look at its juxtaposition (jux-ta-position, Rule #1a) to his explanation of the importance of Petunia's blood, then it is very likely intentional. Dumbledore's wording about Lily's blood protection is the key clue. Dumbledore is now very specific in Book 5 that the blood protection must come through Lily's line – and that Petunia is the last of that line. Because the spell was cast by Lily, apparently James' relations would not suffice. Does this mean that there could still be some relations on Harry's father's side around after all? How does that fit in with Sirius' comment in Book 3 about "the last Potter"? We don't know, so our best advice is CONSTANT VIGILANCE!

COULD CROOKSHANKS BE AN ANIMAGUS?

Even before Book 5 hit the shelves, people were speculating whether Crookshanks could possibly be an Animagus. That was based primarily on his being so intelligent, coupled with his uncanny ability to communicate with Padfoot. Although we don't know for sure, WWP is fairly convinced that Crookshanks is a part Kneazle (reference *Fantastic Beasts*).

If Crookshanks were an Animagus, it would seem that Padfoot should have recognized him as one. In Book 3, Sirius called Crookshanks one of the smartest "of his kind." It is unlikely Sirius would have called him that if his "kind" were human. A less definitive but highly logical reason that Crookshanks is not an Animagus was made quite clear by J.K.R.. Ron commented in Book 3 that Animagi parading as pets is highly deceptive and not at all acceptable behavior for a good guy. Unless Animagi can change gender when they transform, we also cannot imagine that Crookshanks *(he)* would be hanging out in the girl's dorm after what we saw happen to Ron in Book 5 (tee-hee).

The "coincidental" description of Mundungus Fletcher was most likely done by J.K.R. with the specific purpose of teasing us. However, it now has people wondering As this is a magical world, it is possible that there could be some tie between Crookshanks and Mundungus Fletcher. Nonetheless, we are absolutely positive that Crookshanks is **not** Mundungus. Our proof is from Chapter 5 {"Order of the Phoenix"}, where everyone, including Dung, himself, is sitting around the table as Crookshanks settles himself onto Sirius' lap.

——————— *Running Bits* (some tricky ones) ———————

CHAIRS, SINKING
*"She **sank** into the **chair**..."*

2s, BELLS, SILENCE (SECONDS IS A FORM OF 2)
*"Two **seconds** of **ringing silence**..."*

Hints

✳ Items of Intrigue ✳

MR. TIBBLES If you were one of the few who wondered who the Mr. Tibbles was that warned Mrs. Figg, we can guess that you probably haven't worn out your set of Harry Potter books (yet). Harry not only knows Mr. Tibbles, but has seen more than enough of him already. Upon careful reading, you will notice that Tibbles was stationed under a car, and when all the excitement happened, he bounded off. Our Rememberit Quill just scribbled... ⚑ *If you're not up to scratch, you can paw through Book 1, Chapter 3 {"The Vanishing Glass"} for the answer.* ✍

SOMETHING IMPORTANT For being late at night, there was certainly a lot of activity in Magnolia Crescent... like something down the street shortly after the Dementor attack. Was it something important? No, it was just...

DUDLEY'S ATTACK Did HP Sleuths wonder the same thing Harry wondered after the Dementors attacked Dudley? Are you curious about Big D's demons?

✳ Secrets and Concealed Clues ✳

PECK OF CLUES You may think that Uncle Vernon was a bit owl-pecked but we want to know how many pickled peppers did Uncle Vernon pack...uh pick? If you think we're just being childish, then you might want to unpack your *Philological Stone*, and take a quick peek at the nursery rhymes on your reading list.

THE PETUNIA PARADOX What's with Petunia? You couldn't help but notice that she knew a bit more about wizardry than she's been letting on. She even used the (gasp!) "W" word. However, it's not just what she said that got our attention – it's what she didn't say and how she reacted. There were several other huge clues buried in that scene, the least of which was her highly suspicious, "jerky" explanation about the wizard prison. Consider who was more confused about everything that was going on – Petunia or Harry?

TWO BYE TOUS The WWP Sleuthoscope is doubling back, hoping to slyly reinforce its warning. The number two is a huge running bit and is one of the biggest clues in Book 5. HP Sleuths should be carefully researching and transcribing all sightings of two onto your detective parchments (hope you have enough ink!). From a literary perspective, we can't help but think of the biggest "two" we know. Look on your HP Sleuth reading list for a person with a "two" in his name, and review his works for multiple ideas. But who needs literature? There are some monster clues buried in those twos, so make sure you check every corner of Book 5 where the twos are hiding and watch carefully for logical links. If you find some mates, they probably will help you discover the secret. The biggest help we can give you is to remind you of our new Rule #1 corollary: jux-ta-position!

Chapter 3 Clues

(THE ADVANCE GUARD)

FAQs

WHAT'S THE DIFFERENCE BETWEEN A METAMORPHMAGUS AND AN ANIMAGUS?

Both Metamorphmagi and Animagi are people who have the ability to transfigure. The primary difference seems to be that one is a human-to-human transformation and the other is a human-to-animal transformation – although that is not confirmed. For instance, Tonks can change her appearance rather dramatically, but as far as we know, she retains a human form. Another big difference is that the Metamorphmagi are born with the natural ability to alter their features without any training, while Animagus wannabes have to diligently study highly-advanced transfiguration techniques, which they may never be able to master.

WHAT IS THE DIFFERENCE BETWEEN DISILLUSIONMENT AND INVISIBILITY?

Alert HP Sleuths had already known about Disillusionment Charms from *Fantastic Beasts*. However, we did not know exactly how they worked until Book 5. Unlike the Invisibility Cloak, the Disillusionment Charm doesn't make you invisible – it just makes you blend in with the background. You take on the appearance of whatever is around you. So, it isn't perfect. If you get too close to someone, it will be obvious, and if you move around a lot, people would notice the distortion in the background. It probably looks as if the background is shifting in the same way the Romulan "cloaking devices" from Star Trek cause a ripple in space. (Hint – if you're not a Trekkie, it may help to know a few chameleons.)

WAS TONKS THE LAST AUROR SELECTED FROM HOGWARTS?

In Chapter 29 {"Careers Advice"}, Professor McGonagall told Harry that they hadn't selected an Auror candidate from Hogwarts in the last three years. She also described how Aurors have to take an extra three years of training. That means, if the person who was selected three years ago is now an Auror, that person would have just completed the extra training, and qualified this year. However, Tonks has already been an Auror for a year, plus she sounded a bit apologetic about it – as if it took her even longer than some people. So, it doesn't seem as if she was the last (we wonder who was).

Running Bits (some tricky ones)

2s, HEADS (HURT)
"...*two* lumps on his **head**..."

ROUND
"...*three hundred and sixty degrees* visibility..."

BUBBLES, COLOR (PINK)
"...**bubble**-gum pink."

Hints

✳ Items of Intrigue ✳

PODMORE CLUES One of the members of the Advance Guard was Sturgis Podmore. If you think carefully, you should be able to remember where you've seen that name before. Our Quill just scrawled... *Going through Chapter 8 of Book 2 may help, but don't go losing your head over it or you may be the guest of honor at the next Deathday party.*

DEDALUS DIGGLE Another member of the Advance Guard was Dedalus Diggle. The direct path to any clues in his first name is through mythology (note slight spelling difference) and also to *Portrait of the Artist as a Young Man*, by James Joyce (on your HP Sleuth suggested reading list).

TONKS Nymphadora Tonks has a Muggle father. His name is Ted. We do know of another Ted from Chapter 1 of Book 1. *Don't go reading too much into this news item — all we have to go on is Rule #3.*

MISSING KEY We don't feel as if we were given enough information about the way the door to Harry's room opened. Consider if there may be a clue locked in there somewhere.

SHACKLEBOLT The name "Kingsley Shacklebolt" conjures up images of bound servitude – yet his shackles may have "unusual" restraints. If you suddenly encountered a very large, dark, bald, magical person with an incredibly deep voice and an earring in one ear, what would you ask him?

✳ Secrets and Concealed Clues ✳

NOISE HINTS We have some suspicions about the (seemingly normal) creakings and gurglings Harry hears in the Dursley house. "Gurgling" sounds scarily familiar. If nothing else, they're important as running bits.

TRUNKS AND TONKS AND TRICKY IMAGES This one is just too much for the WWP Sleuthoscope. It has just gone all pink around the edges from trying to keep from bouncing off the walls. The whole scene where Tonks was helping Harry peck has it so worked up, it acts as if it's going to burst! There seem to be several *major* clues there. You may want to reflect on your list of running bits while keeping in mind key events from the plot of Book 5.

METAMORPHMAGUS Again, several hair-raising clues here. Tonks never explained how wizards find out if they are a Metamorphmagus. You may want to ask if they start out by making funny faces in the mirror, or do they just wake up one day and discover that their hair has grown three inches overnight?

Chapter 4 Clues

FAQs

WHY IS IT CALLED "GRIMMAULD PLACE"?

You may have recognized the "Grim" in Grimmauld Place. However, did you take it the rest of the way? This is not just tricky, it's a jump out and yell "Boo!" Rowlinguistic. It is at least a *quadruple* pun. Here are the meanings that we have (thus far) deduced. Note - they do hold clues:

Grim	=	Death omen
Grimm auld Place	=	"A grim old place"
Grimm	=	Grimm fairy tales
Grimm	=	Grimm's Law of philology (from Jacob Grimm)

WHAT IS A "SKIRTING BOARD" AND WHY IS THAT IMPORTANT?

When Harry first entered Grimmauld Place, he was a bit confused, and some readers may have been too. Harry hears something "behind the skirting board," and U.S. readers who have the UK version would probably not have understood what that was. The U.S. version clarifies it to mean *baseboard*. However, *skirting/skirt* is a one of the basic running bits that is scampering throughout Book 5, so it is important that HP Sleuths know about this first (and critical) use of the running bit (see Hints below).

WHY ARE THE TWINS ALLOWED TO APPARATE AND WHY DON'T THEY HAVE TO FINISH SCHOOL?

Gred and Forge may act like baboons, but they are really talented wizards. The kind of magic required for their masterpieces of mirth is quite advanced, although according to Hermione, their talents may not be what you would call "traditional." In Chapter 7 {"Bagman and Crouch"} of Book 4, Bagman was highly impressed with their fake wands, which were even able to fool Mrs. Weasley (who should have known to expect them). Then, in Book 5, not only was Professor Flitwick delighted with their Portable Swamp, but they even received a compliment from Hermione about their fireworks and Headless Hats.

Although Fred and George may have only squeaked by with a few OWLS, we suspect that is because they learned what *they* considered most useful – which, of course, was anything tied to making money (and mayhem). The real-world equivalent to that would be the difference between someone who teaches himself to be an expert computer wiz vs. someone who studies for a Ph.D. in Literature. That is why the twins were able to pass that difficult Apparating exam "with Distinction," even though Charlie had to take his twice. (We suspect that the twins may have already had an "understanding" of how to Apparate long before they went for training and testing.)

A wizard is qualified to test for their Apparating License at the age of 17 – just like a Muggle could go for their automobile Operator's License. They only have to be of age; they do not have to be finished with school. We know from Chapter 16 {"The Goblet of Fire"} of Book 4 that Gred and Forge missed the 17-year-old age cut-off by just weeks (poor babies) – proof they had turned 17 in the middle of their sixth year at Hogwarts. That is why they had already taken their Apparating exam even though they were still in school.

According to the system in the magical world, which seems to be similar to Muggle schools in the UK, once you have taken your exams and shown a certain degree of competence, you are considered finished with your education. There is no requirement to continue with school or to take the more advanced NEWT tests. In the case of Gred and Forge, the degree of competency was apparently nominal – given that we know several talented wizards who achieved 12 OWLs, whereas the twins' *combined* OWLs were only half that. Nonetheless, upon receiving their OWLs, the twins are officially qualified as practicing wizards. It's the difference between being at the top of your class vs. the bottom of your class – you still finish school. So, there is nothing keeping them in school except dedication to their House (and a little Pandemonium to ensure they are included in the next edition of *Hogwarts: a History*).

WAS SIRIUS IN SLYTHERIN HOUSE?

After knowing Sirius, it is hard to imagine him a Slytherin. Yet, a bloodline Black was expected to uphold the family tradition in the same way a bloodline Malfoy would do. Based on Phineas' Slytherin affiliation and a few snake trinkets around their house, we are quite sure Sirius' "noble" ancestors were Slytherins. In Book 1, Malfoy told Harry in Madam Malkin's shop that he already *"knew"* he would be in Slytherin – just like the rest of his family. Indeed, the Sorting Hat had *"barely touched his head"* before putting him in Slytherin.

Would Sirius have also been an automatic Slytherin? We don't have any concrete evidence, but we do have a few good hints to dispute it. One is that Sirius has put others' needs before his own (not a very Slytherin-like thing to do). Then there is the overall theme of the Harry Potter septology: "choices." Sirius may not have been perfect, but he never acted out of personal ambition at the cost of others. We know he despised his family's beliefs. Most importantly, in Chapter 9 {"The Woes of Mrs. Weasley"}, we have a hint that may be almost good enough. If you carefully read the conversation about who became prefect and who didn't (among James, Lupin, and Sirius), you will notice that it sounds as if the selection was made from among the three map makers. See our FAQs in Chapter 9 {"The Woes of Mrs. Weasley"} for more on the Hogwarts Prefect system.

—————— *Running Bits* (some tricky ones) ——————

HEMS/SKIRTS (MAYBE MOON/UMBRA)
   *"...**skirting** a large umbrella stand..."*

CEILING, 2s
   *"...high-**ceilinged, twin-bedded room**..."*

—————————— *Hints* ——————————

✴ *Items of Intrigue* ✴

COEURS AND FLEURS We weren't surprised to find Ron and Hermione getting along with each other here the same way they always do (hehe). Nor were we surprised about Bill and Fleur. So, what is going on with the alluring yet absent (curieusement) Fleur?

LITTLE FEETS Harry heard the pattering of little feet behind the skirting board (Ref FAQs) in Grimmauld place, accompanied by a rotting kind of smell. Ron also had something stubborn attach itself to his finger. A quick lookup in *Fantastic Beasts* should be able to clear up that mystery – but you should remember what you uncover, since so much is lurking in that house.

VAMPIRE OR NOT Those fans who are new to HP Sleuthing may not be aware that the biggest controversy surrounding *Professor* Snape is whether he may be a vampire or not (see the "New Bits and Old Bits" section). For those bloodhounds who are tracking that carefully, the most important comment in Book 5 was in this chapter and had to do with his eating habits.

BILL'S OPINION One question we would all like answered is whether Snape is truly a *reformed* Death Eater. Dumbledore has assured Harry that he trusts *Professor* Snape and has evoked Rule #1 in Chapter 37 {"The Lost Prophecy"}. Then again, Bill doesn't like Snape, and that's enough for Ginny. Not much of a consensus, is there? We do have lots of juicy hints, so keep reading...

PORTRAITS VS. PHOTOS As we mentioned in our previous Guide, we had expected the portraits to contribute to Dumbledore's network of information. Even so, it was interesting to see the extent to which the portraits are his eyes and ears. We now know a lot more about what portraits do and what can be done to them. You did see what Mrs. Weasley did to them, didn't you? You can also canvass Chapter 22 {"St Mungo's Hospital for Magical Maladies and Injuries"} for more illustrations of their capabilities. If you want to expand your appreciation for these fine arts, one question you can ask is how a photo (such as one in a newspaper or other photos Harry has encountered) may differ from portraits. We do have an idea

how the magic works. If you can imagine what link there is between the Murtlap in Chapter 15 {"The Hogwarts High Inquisitor"} and what Dumbledore saw in his little machine in Chapter 22, you may get a hint of what magic is behind the portraits.

RON AND HERMIONE If you read carefully, you probably have some questions about what Ron and Hermione were doing before Harry arrived.

MRS. WEASLEY'S STRESS Observant HP Sleuths may have detected that Mrs. Weasley was not as much in the pink, as she is under a bit more stress than usual.

TROLL TRAP Besides being a bit gruesome, there was something really strange about a severed trolls' leg being used as an umbrella stand. However, if you're thinking about that, you are falling right into J.K.R.'s trap by concentrating on the macabre and missing the big clue! She has us tripping over this clue like Tonks was doing – hoping we would never noses. (Perhaps she thinks we are all trolls?)

✳ *Secrets and Concealed Clues* ✳

FUDGE'S FLUNKY Percy said he was living in London to be closer to the Ministry. He can Apparate and he knows how to use Floo Powder. So, why does he "need" to be so close? Was it because he loves the Ministry so much? We're not convinced. You may want to ask Moody if he has any idea why Fudge kept Percy right there in the office – beside him at all times.

PERCY'S LOYALTY Wow! The WWP Sleuthoscope is bounding around – we're just going to have to chain it down (assuming we can catch it). Is Percy just a bit misguided, or has he lost it so badly that he may even be a Death Eater? There are two other possibilities that tie to one big clue! If you read Percy's letter in Chapter 14 {"Percy and Padfoot"}, you might also be able to decipher what his little problem is. Remember – eyes do tell the tail, and all they're telling us here is Rule #2. HP Sleuths know what that means...

YOU-KNOW-WHO Most wizards can't say (let alone hear) the name "Voldemort" without spilling their pumpkin juice. Even though Hermione now has the courage to speak his name, we have some hints in Book 5 that it may not be just blind fear. You should ponder why so many strong-willed wizards (Snape, the Weasleys, McGonagall) have a problem.

PESTS AT #12 The WWP Sleuthoscope is humming as if it thinks we're not going to hear (excuse us... we're gonna have to swat that thing). Hermione remarks about all the nasties that have been breeding in Number Twelve. They weren't that bad, were they?

Chapter 5 Clues

FAQs

IS NEVILLE JUST CLUMSY? IS TONKS JUST CLUMSY?

Nothing is as it first appears in the magical world. Animals can be humans, spiders can be boggarts, and bathrooms can be deadly! We can't trust people to be who they seem, and people can't even trust their own memories. Therefore, when we see someone behaving a bit peculiarly, our assumption is that it is normal for them to be that way in this fantasy world. However, the characters in the Harry Potter books expect humans to have some minimal abilities and what would be considered abnormal mental problems in the Muggle world are abnormal in the magical world as well.

Because we have come to expect it of Neville, we think of his clumsiness as "just Neville" – yet he is considered abnormally clumsy. We now speculate that his condition may have the same cause as Bertha Jorkin's problems – an over-zealous memory charm (or two or three...). Tonks' clumsiness is considered a severe case. Yet, when we see Tonks' problems, we think of it as "just Tonks." We have no confirmation at this time that Neville's condition was caused by magic, however, all evidence points that way. So, if we are suspicious of Neville's nerdiness, should we also be suspicious of Tonks' tripping tendencies?

DOES SILVER HAVE AN EFFECT ON WEREWOLVES LIKE LUPIN?

Werewolf hunters always carry a silver bullet in their hunting supplies. That is because one of the legends about werewolves is they can only be killed by a silver bullet in the heart. However, that is not the case in all werewolf legends, and we haven't yet had any hint if it is true in J.K.R.'s magical world.

Could silver hurt Lupin just by his touching it? Although we don't have absolute proof, we are fairly confident the answer is "No." Lupin sat down to dinner at the table with everyone else, and unless he didn't use any of the plates, cutlery, or cups, he had to have been eating with the "finest" sterling silver of the renaissance.

So, maybe Lupin won't shrivel up from touching a silver plate, but could a sterling silver knife do the trick? Possibly – then again, knives are usually not a good thing. And what about other silvery objects? We have seen theories about Wormtail's silver hand. Just as all that glitters is not gold – silver doesn't necessarily mean sterling. Silver is a very soft metal. A silver hand that is strong enough to crush things, such as the one Wormtail now has, would probably not be sterling silver. It is more likely that it is a magical silver, and if so, it could be even more deadly!

The answer right now is we have no indication that Lupin would need to be killed using a method that differed from other animals or humans. It is certainly possible that he is more resistant to deadly injuries – just as giants have tougher skin. Without further evidence, we will have to consider him to be basically human with a human soul – it's just that he gets a bit more irritable every 28 days...

WHY IS THE VOLDYTHING RESISTANCE CALLED "ORDER OF THE PHOENIX"?

We have not actually been told Dumbledore's specific reason for calling his group "The Order of the Phoenix." We can make a lot of assumptions – such as Dumbledore likes phoenixes or Fawkes plays an important role (maybe striking fear into the enemy). Whenever we are not told information, that is usually a sure sign it's a clue. But we really don't know yet. There isn't anything very meaningful about OOP... that is... unless you're Dung or Luna!

HOW DOES THE FIDELIUS CHARM WORK?

Don't feel badly if the Fidelius Charm is still a bit confusing to you. As Professor Flitwick explained in Book 3, it is complex magic, and not easy to understand.

The simple part is that there is a secret that needs to be kept, and a person to keep the secret – a "Secret Keeper." Once the charm is in place, whatever the person wants to keep secret is not/no longer known to anyone else – even if they would have thought of it previously. So, as was explained by Flitwick in Book 3, even if the Potters were right there in their house, since they were the secret being kept, they could not be seen. Similarly, even though the Order of the Phoenix does have their Headquarters at Grimmauld Place, because it is under the Fidelius Charm, they and the house cannot be seen – even by other wizards who might be looking for them.

Of course, the person who is the Secret Keeper does know the secret, and can tell anyone he wants. Once he divulges the secret, it is known to whoever he tells. However, only the Secret Keeper can divulge it to others. For example, if Dung slipped up and mentioned it to someone else, they could look all they wanted, but they still wouldn't be able to find the Order. Only Dumbledore is capable of letting others in on his Secret. That is why Moody was not able to just tell Harry about Grimmauld Place – he had to show Harry the note that was handwritten by the Secret Keeper, himself (Dumbledore).

So what mischief can a demented house-elf cause? As Dumbledore explained, since Kreacher wasn't the Secret Keeper, he couldn't reveal the Headquarters location to anyone. There also are additional conditions, due to the enchantments binding Kreacher to his duties as a house-elf. Not only could Kreacher not divulge Dumbledore's secret, he also couldn't defy a direct order from Sirius. However, Sirius only instructed Kreacher to not tell anyone about vital information. For instance, Kreacher was probably instructed to not tell anyone who their visitors were or anything they discussed, but it didn't stop Kreacher from mentioning a few personal observations....

That was the loophole Voldemort capitalized on. The simple question of who was emotionally important to Sirius had not specifically been forbidden. It was not covered by the Fidelius Charm or by Kreacher's duty to Sirius, his master. Since there was nothing to stop him, Kreacher told Narcissa about Sirius and Harry. It's the little things that getcha...

WHY IS MUNDUNGUS IN THE ORDER?

He's foul, he's smelly, he's a crook, and he's in the Order of the Phoenix. So, why does Dumbledore have a Dung in the Order? The reason we are given is actually a very logical one. Dumbledore needs to use all the resources he has available (even some more unusual ones) in order to stay informed about whatever Voldemort is up to. We already know that the people who align themselves with Voldemort tend to be a bit unsavory. In fact, there could be evidence that Dung is having no trouble getting in tight with the enemy (see hints below). No better way to keep track of the unsavory types than to hear the gossip first-hand. So, how valuable is Dung's contribution to the Order? How valuable is your silverware?

Running Bits (some tricky ones)

TWISTED/COILING, EYES
  "Screwing up her eyes..."

FROGS/TOADS
  "...Warty Harris..."

Hints

✳ *Items of Intrigue* ✳

DUNG'S DEALINGS When thinking about the person who had been boobytrapping Muggle toilets, HP Sleuths may want to check Rule #3, as well as one of Dung's "business partners."

MINISTRY OFFICERS Combining what we learn here, with the information in Chapter 10 {"Luna Lovegood"}, we now know how long Cornelius Fudge has been in office. We also learn who the former Minister for Magic was, and under what circumstances she left. You can do some checking into her background if you look up Chapter 27 {"Padfoot Returns"} in Book 4. You may want to question if Fudge was an improvement or not.

HAIR-RAISING QUESTION Since "hair" is used as a personality trait, it is difficult to determine if it should have running bit status or not. Either way, are you watching the growing references to hair?

✳ *Secrets and Concealed Clues* ✳

EXTENDABLE EARS Extendable Ears are like highly-concentrated running bits. They have alliteration (doubles), they are described as "snaking through the house," and they are one super-sensitive ear – otherwise known as the better to hear clues with.... (just watch out for grandmothers with pointy teeth).

FW&W Bill jokes about Dumbledore not caring about being demoted – as long as they don't take him off the Chocolate Frog cards. We already stated our opinion about that in our first Guide analysis of Chapter 6 {"The Journey from Platform Nine and Three-quarters"} from Book 1.

TEMPTING CLUE Ag! Have HP Sleuths spotted a clue on the dining table? Given where his head's at, Dung saw it right away (although we're quite sure it wasn't the clue part that got his attention). Not everything in the Black house may be ancient. You may want to review your schoolbooks to see how it may be possible that the Black family could still have access to valuable resources.

BAGMAN AND HIS DEPARTMENT We noticed Ludo Bagman seemed to be missing. It appears that others may have noticed too.... Yet, did you get a look at his department at the Ministry in Chapter 7 {"Ministry of Magic"}? That reinforces people's opinions about his leadership abilities and may be saying a lot about what is happening in there now.

GOBLIN NAME As we surmised in our first Guide, the goblin issue is a sticky one, and so far, the goblins have not chosen sides. However, those HP Sleuths who are well-versed in Norse mythology (on your HP Sleuth reading list) may not be optimistic about the chances for peace with the goblins or that goblin leader– especially considering that we were prevented from hearing more by Rule #2.

BARELY A GLIMPSE Did you spot what was on the table as the Order was cleaning up? Mrs. W pulled it right out from under our noses to tease us. Just consider that a visual Rule #2. A couple of possibilities are to think about what Hermione told us in Chapter 5 {"The Dementor"} of Book 3, or maybe a mention by one of the Professors in Book 1 (you may kneed to consult your running bits.)

DINING AT #12 Note who sat at the dinner table and when they departed.

Chapter 6 Clues

FAQs

WHAT DOES "TOUJOURS PUR" MEAN?

The literal translation of "Toujours Pur" is *Always Pure*. The translation that is closer to the implied connotation is *Forever Pure*. The implication is almost one of an oath, and reinforces the concept of superiority through purity of blood.

WHAT ARE THE POSSIBLE ROOTS TO THE HOUSE OF BLACK?

There are too many holes for us to do a verifiable genealogy of the immediate Black family members we know – let alone those who are more distantly related. For this chart, we have made the assumption that Sirius was being specific when he called someone a cousin (unqualified) vs. a "removed" cousin. We also started with the premise that Nigellus was, indeed, Phineas' last name. We don't know Sirius' mother's name (first or last)! She said the house was her ancestors', and they implied intermarriage, so it is possible that she may have been a Black, herself. We just don't know.

When trying to determine Arthur Weasley's relationship to Sirius, what helps us there is that a *second-cousin once removed* is very specific. We can at least illustrate the relationship. However, even when assuming that Arthur branches from the Nigellus line, there are still two valid scenarios. This is one best-guess representation of the Black family genealogy based on known information.

Possible Roots to the House of Black

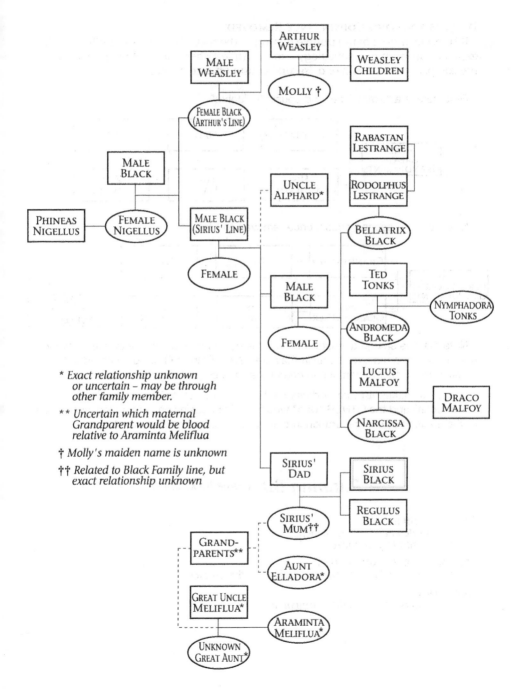

* Exact relationship unknown
  or uncertain – may be through
  other family member.

** Uncertain which maternal
  Grandparent would be blood
  relative to Araminta Meliflua

† Molly's maiden name is unknown

†† Related to Black Family line, but
  exact relationship unknown

WHAT IS A SECOND COUSIN ONCE REMOVED?

If HP Sleuths are having trouble getting at the root of that Black family tree, this explanation from our genealogy expert, Anne Fisher, may help you to visualize the complex relationship of a "second cousin once removed."

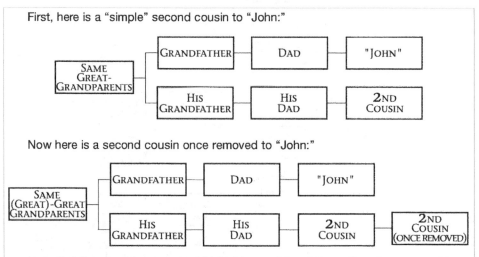

First, here is a "simple" second cousin to "John:"

Now here is a second cousin once removed to "John:"

Note that the shared ancestor of "John" is considered Great-Grandparents *to him*, but to his "once removed" cousin they are "GREAT-Great-Grandparents" (due to the addition of another generation in one of the lines but not the other).

In case it makes it more understandable, the two "Dads" would be first cousins, while "John" and the OTHER "Dad" would be first cousins once removed (again, due to the addition of one generation in one of the lines but not the other).

Running Bits (some tricky ones)

PAIRS/DOUBLE
> "...*double*-ended, colour-coded..."
> "All thanks to you, **mate**..."

SPIDERY, TABLEWARE, CHEST
> "...*spiders* as large as **saucers** lurking in the **dresser**..."

CRACKING
> "...the glass covering them **smashed**."

Hints

✳ *Items of Intrigue* ✳

THE GHOUL The description of the ghoul bothered us a bit. Would you say they were being literal?

LINKED NAMES Before Book 5, we had begun seeing a pattern with some names that were cropping up. Now that we have ploughed through Book 5, we have grown quite certain that there is probably a relationship. What do these names have in common?

Basil	Fleur	Narcissa	Petunia
Daisy	Hogwarts	Olive	Pomona
Firenze	Lavender	Padma	Poppy
Florean	Lily	Pansy	Rose
Florence	Myrtle	Perenelle	Violet

MORE LINKED NAMES Book 5 also illuminated a whole new set of given names that should be explored. We see that these names definitely share common origins, which may help solve some of the mysteries in J.K.R.'s universe. The etymologies of these given names definitely hint at intriguing mysteries. What do these names have in common?

Alphard	Regulus (this is a tricky one)
Andromeda	Rabastan (this is a trickier one)
Bellatrix	Sirius

YET MORE LINKED NAMES This is a wordplay relationship that may tell us something very interesting about Figgy. It's not solid evidence, but it does raise some interesting questions. (Hope it's not what it looks like for her sake!) What do these names have in common?

Arabella	Constellation
Bellatrix	Elladora

GINNY'S POWER We have had our eyes on Ginny right from Book 1. In our first Guide, we said "We think she will have a big role in Book 5 – no longer a weak character." Did you see several examples of "little" Ginny's wizarding skills and (even more important) an endorsement by the twins?

BLACK FAMILY MEMBERS HP Sleuths should have been taking very careful notes as Sirius described the background on each member of the family. One thought that should be flitting through the heads of HP Sleuths is that it's not always which Dark Wizards are on that pureblood tapestry, but which ones are not....

PRECIOUSS HEIRLOOMS There were a few Black family artifacts that we considered important. One little item in particular seemed significant, but had vanished. We were specifically informed that it was salvaged from the dustbins.

✳ Secrets and Concealed Clues ✳

THE BOX The WWP Sleuthoscope looks like it is falling asleep on the job...good thing too, because this is a deadly clue! Our favorite Black family heirloom was a very charming box. Where did that box go? What could you do with it? It should remind you of something. We advise HP Sleuths to review Book 1 as well as your mythology for similar effects. ✦ *You're asleep on the case if you can't get this noteworthy clue from the end of Book 1.* ✐

GRIM PLACE WWP Sleuthoscope is stirring from it's sleep and creeping around. Grimmauld Place conjures up images of the classic Gothic mansion. It was big, old, and without other people around, it could have been a bit unnerving. The Kreacher guy didn't help either, but at least he was usually off in the attic or somewhere. We are not surprised that Sirius didn't like it. Even though Harry didn't mind, did you notice that it still gave him weird images as he lay in bed?

SLEUTH FORENSICS With all the nasty creatures that seem to have been infesting the Black House, it may not have been surprising to find dead things. However, as highly-trained detectives, HP Sleuths should investigate *all* (even the smallest) deaths.

CREATURE WEAPONS The WWP Sleuthoscope is starting to get very restless. It's having so much trouble keeping still that we had to squash it. With all the multi-legged items and weird creatures in Grimmauld Place (not to mention a certain house-elf), it seemed more like a menagerie than a house. It was, indeed, a great inspiration for Harry's weird dreams of the creature weapons. Kreacher did turn out to be pretty deadly, didn't he? Thankfully, he's not much of a threat on his own. (We'd hate to see a clone army of him.) Worse still, an army of something Hagrid might dream up could be a problem. Good thing Hagrid doesn't really teach weapons – he'd probably like the deadliest ones best!

TAPESTRY SECRETS We consider the Black family tapestry to be highly significant (sorry Sirius). Not only could it be important due to the fact that it has seven centuries of information about wizard history buried in it, but HP Sleuths should think carefully about whether it might not be hiding *other* deep, dark secrets. It all comes down to Phineas and his tale (which he has yet to tell).

KREACHER KLUES The WWP Sleuthoscope is playing lightly with the Van de Graaff. We feel like we're watching "Kreacher features" when we see the description of Kreacher shuffling across the floor (you could think Mel Brooks too). It should also remind J.R.R. Tolkien fans of a slimy creature who was deceiving two masters at once. In fact, you may want to consider Fred's words to Hermione during the scene in the drawing room.

Chapter 7 Clues

(THE MINISTRY OF MAGIC)

FAQs

IN WHAT WAYS ARE THE MINISTRY OF MAGIC OFFICES LIKE A MUGGLE OFFICE?

Mr. Weasley would be fascinated to find out that his Ministry of Magic office is an underground version of a typical Muggle office complex. By reading carefully, you will discover that the Atrium is on eighth floor where there is a bank of lifts (elevators) just like in a high-rise. The "golden symbols" that keep changing on the ceiling are the magical equivalent of a stock ticker board or a corporate notice board. The inter-departmental memos are more similar to how memos used to be delivered in the ancient days (before computers). But if anyone wants proof that magic can't solve the problems of the world, we now see that even the Ministry workers are cursed with cubicles for workspace. (sigh)

WHAT IS THE WIZENGAMOT?

In Anglo-Saxon medieval times, the powerful and learned people of the land would assemble to made decisions and offer advice. This assembly (many of whom were elders) was referred to as a witenagemot. J.K.R. has done a little pun thing and created a wizard version. How Harry attracted enough notoriety to warrant such an audience can only be explained by Draco Malfoy: *"Famous Harry Potter."*

WHY WAS HARRY TRIED IN COURTROOM 10?

The first question that needs to be answered is why Harry was even *in* a courtroom? Harry was summoned to a "disciplinary hearing" as stated in the letter he received from the "Improper Use of Magic Office." According to the information that Mr. Weasley had been given, the hearing was to take place in the office of Amelia Bones, the Head of the Department of Magical Law Enforcement. That seems to have been standard practice for a violation such as this – based on the reaction from the adults. Instead, Harry's hearing actually took place in a criminal courtroom. Just as Muggle children would not be tried by the same courts as an adult, it was not expected that Harry's infringement would have been overheard by the entire Wizengamot. As Harry estimated about 50 Wizengamot members present, it required the use of a large room. Assembling all those judges in that particular courtroom was assuredly intended as intimidation.

WHY DID THEY CHANGE THE TIME OF HARRY'S HEARING?

We can answer that with just one word: Dumbledore.

Without Dumbledore, Harry would surely have been convicted. This is very Kafkaesque and arbitrary – in which laws of government are "altered" on the whims of individuals. It is depressing that Fudge would have allowed such a thing – let alone have encouraged it.

——————— *Running Bits* (some tricky ones) ———————

POKING, SHARP, SPINDLY, FALLING (SLIPPING)
  "...impaling the slip of paper on a small brass spike."

SPOTS
  "A small, smudged sign..."

——————————— *Hints* ———————————

✳ *Items of Intrigue* ✳

6-2-4-4-2 That wasn't just a random number that Mr. Weasley dialed to get down to the Ministry of Magic. Just like so many things in Book 5, there is at least a double meaning if you look at your alpha-numerics. If you're having trouble, please check your number and try your call again.

WIZARD IN SCARLET Harry saw the mundane side of an Auror's life: paperwork. He also saw yet another customer for Delilah. We don't see much of that wizard in scarlet, but from his actions at the end, we think we know whose side he's on.

CHICKEN Bob's fire-breathing chicken might have reminded HP Sleuths of some other nasty critters of Hagrid's and even a possible new species that was mentioned by Newt Scamander in his book. If you recall, we never did find out where those came from. Is this a new fad (we thought it was illegal), or is it normal for wizards to be creating all these experimental creatures?

SOUNDS OF MAGIC Has it hit you yet that Book 5 is a very *noisy* book? Previously we had mostly banging, but gongs, clanging, ringing, ticking, rattling and other things are propagating. Those are the kinds of sounds that put our nerves on edge.

REINFORCEMENTS AND THE UNEXPLAINED Did you see the color of the transportation fires in the fireplaces at the Ministry of Magic? In case you didn't realize it, that was a Rule #1. We also see many symbols on the ceiling. Those are a Rule #2.

✳ *Secrets and Concealed Clues* ✳

AUROR HEADQUARTERS Harry got to see what the Auror Headquarters looks like in the Ministry of Magic. Did you find it impressive? The most interesting thing we spotted was the sign.

SOGGY CLUES The WWP Sleuthoscope is acting as if it's about to spill something important. All those regurgitating toilets are spewing out messages to us about some colossal clues. Hope HP Sleuths are documenting all this.

Chapter 8 Clues

FAQs

WHY DID DUMBLEDORE AVOID EYE CONTACT WITH HARRY?

It doesn't take NEWT-level detective work to notice that Dumbledore was avoiding looking at Harry throughout most of Book 5. The reason Dumbledore was being so shifty was because Voldemort was being such a pain in the head to Harry.

In Chapter 24 ["Occlumency"}, Harry learned that eye-contact is a key. Where have we heard that before? Didn't Imposter Moody mention it in his lessons too? Seems that is an essential part of those spells which target the brain. Normally, Voldything would have to make direct eye contact in order for his mind-controlling spells to work. But, since he has a direct mind-meld to Harry via the scar, he doesn't need to make eye contact with him – he just turns on his Voldy charm to make the link. However, eye contact is necessary for people other than Harry, and even observing the eyes of those affected is revealing.

Considering that Voldemort is actually sharing Harry's brain, if Harry, in turn, makes eye contact with someone else, then Voldemort can just look right through Harry – directly into the mind of whoever Harry is eyeing. If you were Dumbledore, you might not want to look Harry in the eye either!

There was one more nasty side effect of this. We need to ask how far Voldything can go in controlling Harry's thoughts. We have already witnessed Voldemort inducing Harry to "see" things that are not real (such as Sirius in the Department of Mysteries).

This is what Dumbledore's concerned about. This is why Harry needs Occlumency lessons – to learn how to block Voldemort from sharing his brain.

CAN FIGGY REALLY SEE DEMENTORS?

Figgy didn't fool all the Wizengamot, and she didn't fool Harry. We know she didn't see the Dementors, but we don't know why. We assume it was because she arrived late from trying to beat the crap out of Dung. However, she gave an accurate account of the order of events as they occurred – including the details about the number of times that Harry attempted his Patronus spell. We never witnessed Harry telling anyone what happened that night, so how would she know if she wasn't there to see it? It is likely that Harry could have discussed it with the adults and they would have informed Dumbledore. But that is only speculation.

We are told that Squibs can see Dementors. We are told that Figgy is a Squib. Yet, she obviously did not see them that night. So, did someone brief her about what happened so she could describe it at the Hearing, or did she witness the attack but not truly see the Dementors after all? The jury is still out on that one.

———— *Running Bits* (some tricky ones) ————

EYES (BULGING)
*"....she wore a **monocle**..."*

MOUTH (OPEN), SWELLING, HEARTS
*"...**opened his mouth** to speak, but his **swollen heart**..."*

DUNG
*"...are anything other than **bilge**..."*

———————— *Hints* ————————

✳ *Items of Intrigue* ✳

SUMMONING STATEMENT Dumbledore offered to summon Dobby as a witness. HP Sleuths should consider whether that was one of Dumbledore's figures of speech.

WHINGING WIZARDS Do we believe the statement that there are no other wizards living around Privet Drive? HP Sleuths who took careful notes during court have transcribed how we were informed the Ministry of Magic is keeping very close watch on Number Four. They should know, shouldn't they?

C. OSWALD FUDGE Fudge is an Oswald. Are we surprised? U.S. readers may be thinking of a certain assassinator when they hear that name. However, it is more likely that you will find the correct Oswald if you search the Nazi ranks for a particular Brit with ties to one of J.K.R.'s personal heroines.

BLUE CLUES This book can make you blue. However, there are blues and then there are specific blues. Have you seen the clues?

✳ *Secrets and Concealed Clues* ✳

"THE HEARING" The WWP Sleuthoscope is trying very hard to be silent. This chapter is called "The Hearing" – sounds to us like a running bit. Are HP Sleuths hearing what we're hearing? Hope there's nothing wrong with your ears.

PERCY CLUE It appears from the court record that Percy is just plain Percy. But that still makes us think about Perseus from Greek Mythology. Knowing that we have a "Rabastan" among us, the legend of Perseus should be on your must-read list.

DUMBLEDORE'S NAMES The HP Hintoscope is surreptitiously humming Christmas carols.... We knew there was more to Dumbledore than just buzzing around, but we now know he has several unique middle names. It's not Percy Weasley who has the King Arthur/Holy Grail tie, but it is Dumbledore, himself! HP Sleuths may want to revisit that legend, but the name that has the HP Hintoscope all worked up is "Brian." Knowing that J.K.R. is a Monty Python fan, and that there are several references in Book 5 with pious origins, HP Sleuths might want to check out a Monty Python movie from your Suggested Supplies.

A CHAIR BY ANY OTHER NAME The WWP Sleuthoscope is fidgeting in it's seat. Must be a fairly big clue....better get the *Philological Stone* to help. Nice chair, Harry – if you don't mind staying awhile. If you sit for awhile with your mythology references, you may find that this chair (or its twin) has a bit of legend surrounding it, along with other important seats in Egyptian mythology. That rattling and binding action does give us the willies. We see that Dumbledore prefers the more comfortable (and friendlier) ones – although he likes to draw them up himself.

DUMBLEDORE'S LUCK If you are an experienced HP Sleuth, you know that Dumbledore's "lucky mistakes" (such as showing up early) have something to with Rule #3.

Chapter 9 Clues

(THE WOES OF MRS. WEASLEY)

FAQs

WHO ARE THE MEMBERS OF THE ORDER OF THE PHOENIX?

Just like with Voldemort's Death Eaters, we don't know all of Dumbledore's members of the Order of the Phoenix. Here is the list of known current and past members.

Sirius Black	Past/Current	Marlene McKinnon	Past
Edgar Bones	Past	Dorcas Meadowes	Past
Caradoc Dearborn	Past	Alastor Moody	Past/Current
Dedalus Diggle	Past/Current	Peter Pettigrew	Past
Elphias Doge	Past/Current	Sturgis Podmore	Past/Current
Albus Dumbledore	Past/Current	Lily Potter	Past
Aberforth (Dumbledore)	Past/Current(?)	James Potter	Past
Benjy Fenwick	Past	Fabian Prewett	Past
Arabella Figg *(Old Crowd)*	Past/Current	Gideon Prewett	Past
Mundungus Fletcher *(Old Crowd)*	Past/Current	Kingsley Shacklebolt	Current
		Severus Snape	Current
Rubeus Hagrid	Past/Current	Nymphadora Tonks	Current
Hestia Jones	Current	Emmeline Vance	Past/Current
Alice Longbottom	Past	Arthur Weasley	Current
Frank Longbottom	Past	Bill Weasley	Current
Remus Lupin	Past/Current	Charlie Weasley	Current
Minerva McGonagall	Current	Molly Weasley	Current

(All members listed as "Past" were killed – except one rat.)

WHAT IS "MOLLYCODDLING"?

"Mollycoddling" is a real word and is simply someone who pampers people excessively. Not our Molly, the saber-toothed tiger lady, is it?

HOW DOES THE PREFECT SYSTEM WORK?

There is a male and female Prefect chosen for each House – from fifth year on up. That means, just for the fifth-year class, there are two Prefects, each, for Gryffindor, Ravenclaw, Hufflepuff, and Slytherin. There are also two Prefects per House for sixth and seventh-year classes. Head Boy and Head Girl are chosen only in the final (seventh) year. Nowhere are we told, yet, if someone can be replaced as Prefect in a later year if they messed up. Additionally, It would seem logical that it would be quite difficult (if not impossible) to become Head Boy or Girl if you did not make it to Prefect. However, we seem to have had a situation like that at Hogwarts (see Hints below).

Using the evidence that Tonks gave us about why she hadn't been chosen as

Prefect, we can conclude that the Head of House has a major say in the selection. We also know that Headmaster Dumbledore informed Harry in {"The Lost Prophecy"} that it was *his* decision not to appoint Harry as Prefect. It is reasonable to conclude that the Heads of House nominate the candidate(s), and that the Headmaster makes the final approval.

──────── *Running Bits* (some tricky ones) ────────

PADLOCK, CHAINS
"....was **bound** to pick you.."

SMELLS, LEGS, NOSE (HURT)
"...**sniffing** at a chicken-**leg** with **what remained of his nose**..."

9 OF 10
"...**nine months,**' said Harry, counting them off **on his fingers**..."

──────────── *Hints* ────────────

✳ *Items of Intrigue* ✳

MAGICAL BRETHREN Many people would love to be surrounded by adoring creatures who happily traipsed along in their wake. However, the Fountain of Magical Brethren should have given HP Sleuths a feel for why there is so much friction in the magical world. Everything else we have seen in the Ministry of Magic is a cover-up for something deadly. What about the image of gleeful statues in the fountain? What is festering under the surface?

OLD MEMBERS Moody's picture of the "Order of the Phoenix" members hinted at several clues. Did you notice how the rat always seems to worm his way into the middle of things? Where have we seen the Prewetts, the McKinnons, and the Bones before Book 5, and what do we know about them? We see the Rememberit Quill has been doodling... *In Chapter 4 of Book 1, Hagrid mentioned them ... oh, you looked...drat, I shouldn'ta told ya' that.*

CHICKEN JOKE Why did the chicken cross the road? To go on a date with a skrewt. (Or was it to avoid being dinner at Grimmauld Place?)

RECOGNIZING REALITY Everyone thought that Sirius was confused about whether Harry is himself or his dad. Fudge thought that Dumbledore was making things up. Everyone thought that Luna was loony. What do you think?

TONKS AT HOGWARTS Tonks and Harry have more in common than not being Prefect – such as a little problem with rules.... Tonks explained how she wasn't selected for Prefect in *her House*. HP Sleuths are probably aware that she left out one piece of important information there.

HOUSES If HP Sleuths look carefully at what Sirius says about Lupin being Prefect, it does imply something about what House the three of them were in. Where does that leave Peter?

MOLLY' MOTHERING The dead bodies of all of the people Molly cared about were being simulated by the boggart. Did you see who appeared? Maybe it was nothing, but did you see who was missing?

✳ Secrets and Concealed Clues ✳

MALFOY'S POCKET We had already figured that Fudge had certain weaknesses. Looks like Lucius Malfoy has all the figures stuffed in his pocket, doesn't it?

MAD-EYE The WWP Sleuthoscope is glowing electric blue – could it be that it wants to be noticed? What have HP Sleuths noticed about Mad-Eye's magical eye? This is a septology biggie – although you have to look a little beyond this chapter if you want to see the biggest clue.

ABERFORTH Yeah! We finally got to see Dumbledore's brother, Aberforth. uh...guess not...or did we?

JAMES AS HEAD BOY Weren't we told in Chapter 4 {"Keeper of the Keys"} of Book 1 that James was Head Boy? Since we now know for sure he wasn't a Prefect, that would leave only one way for him to become Head Boy.

PAST MEMBER OF OOP If you claim there was a murder, you've got to have a body. Of course, in J.K.R.'s world, that wouldn't necessarily be enough. However, if there's no body, HP Sleuths should know better than to assume there was a murder – no matter how reliable the source (Rule #4)

Chapter 10 Clues

(LUNA LOVEGOOD)

The WWP Sleuthoscope is slowing turning as it tries to keep on its brakes. It's time for HP Sleuths to go metric. There's still plenty of 12s for all you 12 fans, but in Book 5, we were bowled over by the number 10. This chapter is one of the most important chapters to the septology. We advise HP Sleuths to read it several times (even upside-down and backwards if you have to). Some of the biggest hints are hiding in here.

FAQs

WAS THERE NEW EVIDENCE ABOUT OUR LUPIN-JAMES SPECULATION?

If you don't know about our Lupin-James theory, we speculated in our first Guide that Remus and James may have switched places using a Switching Spell before Voldemort's attack. Here are some of the points where people have had confusion.

A Switching Spell could be used as the ultimate disguise to switch two humans. The reason the switching spell would work is that only the body parts are switched – the internal person stays the same. Since werewolfism is caused by a bite (a person is not born that way), it makes sense that it would transfer with the body parts.

If you dispute our theory based on the wand shadows in Book 4, we were going by Dumbledore's description of them in Chapter 36 {"The Parting of the Ways"}. J.K.R. specified that the shadows were only *"a kind of reverse echo" (Dumbledore repeated the word "echo," Rule #3)*. The wand echoes are *not* the soul of the person – just a bounced "image." It would be similar to the portraits, which always look like the person did at the time they were painted.

As to the *reason* for the switch – we were implying that if the "Potters" were somehow important to the existence of wizards in the same way Harry is, then it would be imperative that James stay alive and safe (and under wraps) *at any cost*. We were **NOT** implying that James was a coward or that he was saving his own skin! We also think that if our theory is true, he could somehow have been getting glimpses of Harry all these years the same way that Sirius did in Book 3.

Now in Book 5, we have four incidents that keep us alert – all having to do with Lupin touching Harry. In this chapter, look how Lupin shook hands with everyone else but only gave Harry *"a clap on the shoulder."* In Chapter 24 {"Occlumency"}, there is an identical situation in which Lupin, again, shook everyone's hands and all we are told is that he *talked* to Harry. However, in Chapter 35 {"Beyond the Veil"}, as Harry dashed toward the Veil, Lupin grabbed him firmly around the chest. If we are right about the switch, normally that could have been dangerous – given Harry's Legilimens link (think about what happened in Chapter 27 {"The Centaur and the Sneak"} when Dumbledore touched him!). In this case, though, Harry's mind was so focused on one thing (*get-to-Sirius!*) that there was no way any other emotion could have eeked out.

41

We still do believe there is *something* going on with Lupin. Remember – his parting words to Harry were *"Keep in touch."*

DID DRACO MALFOY REALLY KNOW ABOUT PADFOOT?

Throughout the whole septology, Draco has been kept quite well informed by dear Daddy. In Book 2, although his father wouldn't tell him everything, he knew a lot of details about the Chamber of Secrets. In Book 3, he knew that Sirius Black was Harry's godfather even before Harry found out. In Book 4, he knew exactly what was going on with the Death Eaters at the World Cup, and was told all about the Triwizard Tournament before arriving at the train.

Sirius explains in "Order of the Phoenix" that Wormtail would have informed Voldemort that Sirius was an Animagus, so the Death Eaters would have also known. There is proof of that in Chapter 36 {"The Only One He Ever Feared"}, when Bellatrix tells Voldything that she was dueling with *"the Animagus Black."* Snape tells Sirius in Chapter 24 {"Occlumency"} that Lucius had recognized him at the train. Therefore, Draco was, indeed, aware that it was Sirius who was bounding along with Harry. We just can't be sure whether Draco shared this information willingly or unwillingly with anyone else (yes, that's a hint).

—————— *Running Bits* (some *tricky ones*) ——————

SPOTS
> *"...aura of distinct **dottiness.**"*

STOMACHS, HEARTS
> *"...sinister look of some diseased **internal organ.**"*

HANDS, SLIDING
> *"...slipped out of her grasp, slid down..."*

————————————— *Hints* —————————————

✳ *Items of Intrigue* ✳

RECOMMENDED READING FOR CHAPTER 10 You should have your Suggested Reading on hand for this chapter. Not only is it a good idea to have all previous Harry Potter books, but you should grab James Joyce – along with Milton, Lewis Carroll, and definitely some crib notes from the Kids' Korner. Even if you barely cracked the spines on most of those in school, a quick look through them would give you some important background.

LUNA CLUES The name "Luna" is, indeed, another loony moon-type name. If you have been diligent with your Classical mythology reading list, you may have run across a certain moon goddess who had some really *big* ancestors. We encourage HP Sleuths to read up on myths surrounding the moon goddess for some more insight into Luna Lovegood. If you recall, she comments to Harry about being "as sane as I am" – and we all know how crazy people get at the full moon...

LUNA'S EYES Those big, unblinking eyes of Luna's are boring into our brains. HP Sleuths who have been studying hard should know that not blinking can be good (think Book 3). You should also be able to recall where we have seen eyes just like those before. ⚡ *You better go for some wand maintenance if you can't remember.* ✒

THE WEATHER We realize northern Scotland isn't a tropical paradise, but you might have noticed that Mother Nature's been in a real temper these last three books.

MOON GODDESS Luna spends a long time just looking at Harry and Ron – you may ask yourself what she sees in either of them. Could it depend on whether the moon has passed by Venus lately?

LUNA'S PERSPECTIVE You probably don't have to be told that Luna Lovegood seems to see the world from a whole different *perspective*. HP Sleuths know that different can often mean better.

I'M NOBODY Neville says "I'm nobody." We say HP Sleuths might want to see what Homer or Emily Dickenson have said about the importance of that (see your Suggested Reading).

ASSYRIA Neville really likes his plant (says he has some big plans for it). Didn't he say that his Uncle brought it back from Assyria? We've heard about Assyria, so why can't we find it on the map? Then again, why can't we find Hogwarts? HP Sleuths may want to start their search with Amnesty International, and then question Uncle Algie's excursions.

THE CONCERT So the WWP Sleuthoscope doesn't give too much away, we will sit on it while we discuss a few more hints that may slip by you. Doris Purkiss and her account about the concert are interesting. Take special note of where it took place. If you are up on your literature, it may help (or it may confuse you more) if you reference Chapters 31 and 34 {"OWLs" and "Department of Mysteries"} – the reference has to do with a work by T.S. Eliot.

✳ Secrets and Concealed Clues ✳

CLUES IN CHAPTER 10 That did it! The WWP Sleuthoscope couldn't contain itself any longer... it started laughing so hysterically that it fell back, slid off the desk, and hit the floor. (oop!) There are some scenes in this chapter that are so packed with clues it could take fifty years for us just to write them all up.... just don't write off Luna. Keep your quill soaked with plenty of ink!

STUBBY BLACK There may be something going on, but what caught our ear was the concert. What happened to Stubby at the concert may also strike a chord with literary buffs, or make you check your running bits for clues. Keep those running bit reference cards handy!

NASTY DEEDS According to the bizarre article in the Quibbler, Fudge has been doing all sorts of nasty things to goblins. He has supposedly been drowning them and dropping them off buildings. Now who would try to do anything like that? *If you slimy sleuths can't find your Book 1 parchments, you may never get to the bottom of this clue.*

BABOON JOKE All this monkeying around should have HP Sleuths going bananas. The baboon joke has a familiar look to it. It seems vaguely reminiscent of a very big mythological deity or a bad planet joke from Book 4 divination. Ron saw it – can you? (Our rude Rememberit Quill is insisting that it wants a look....)

EYES, HEAD, MOUTH Speaking of looking... the three of them sitting there are such a sight. Poor Neville had a little problem with gooey eyes. At least Ginny only got her head covered by the Stinksap. But the worst of the three was Harry, who had to spit out a mouthful of the slimy stinky stuff (gross!). You may not want to get in the line of fire, but it would be worthwhile to try poking around that plant of Neville's a bit.

LUNA'S SLIPPERY QUIBBLER What, besides the name, might be important in that Quibbler? Good thing it slid down onto the floor where Harry could take a look. Oh – that reminds us – we had better pick up our fidgety little Sleuthoscope. Now HP Sleuths can get a long, hard look at that magazine. There's a lot to see in there – so don't tell us we didn't warn you...

TITLE OF THE ARTICLE It would be a good idea for HP Sleuths to scrutinize those Quibbler articles – they're more than just jokes. They're literally clues. Where do you start? We suggest you start with the title and go from there.

FUDGE FOR DESSERT HP Sleuths should bone up on Fudge's unique culinary talents. Maybe he doesn't strike fear into the hearts of goblins, but you might want to be concerned about his appetite for gold.

> Sing a song of Galleons
> What has Fudge got up his sleeve?
> If you think the Quibbler's crazy
> Well, that is what you're supposed to believe.

Chapter 11 Clues

(THE SORTING HAT'S NEW SONG)

FAQs

WHAT DID RON SAY TO NICK?

Ron was a bit insensitive to Nearly-Headless Nick, so with the help of a glare from Hermione, he attempted to make it better. However, with a mouth full of food, what came out was somewhat garbled. This is like a Rorschach* psychological test for language fans (you know – the ones where they show you an ink blot and you have to try to see some kind of creature in there?). Don't get stuck on the letters – just say it out loud and concentrate on the big picture. Learning how to read foodtalk is yet another Book 5 lesson for HP Sleuths. (Note that the words have a bit of a Dudley look to them too.)

Here is what Ron said to Nick and the translation:

Foodtalk: Node iddum eentup sechew
English: No (de), I dun' mean t' upset you

* *(pronounced roar-shack)*

IS THERE SOMETHING SIGNIFICANT ABOUT THIS YEAR'S PASSWORD?

As usual, the passwords contain clues. This year's Gryffindor common room password was: Mimbulus Mimbletonia. As Harry would say, "that's definitely a mouthful!" (hehe) You are probably aware that it was the only password this year. Why was there only one? If you asked the Fat Lady, she'd probably have told you it was so difficult that she figured none of the Slytherins could say it – let alone remember it! If you ask us, we would say either it's a really, really important clue, or J.K.R. thought we needed a lot of time to think. We can assure you that it's probably both. Now, you may need to come face-to-face with a baboon's backside or be hit in the head with some Stinksap (like we were) to get it – but it is a skeleton key to Book 5!

To start you off, here are some derivations of the name. Study these carefully – or the Stinksap might catch you by surprise...

Mimbulus Mimbletonia
Possible Derivations of the Words

Mimbulus
  Nimbus = halo
  Cumulo Nimbus = storm cloud
  Nimble = move (movable)
  Gimble = Jabberwocky (find an annotated *Alice*)
  *Mimulus = Figwort family = monkey flower
  Wimble = bore, extract, helical, auger

Mimbulus Mimbletonia
MM = double, twain
Mimble-Wimble = spell is ineffective
    (per HP Trading Card Game/Nintendo)
Wimble-Wamble = roll about as walking

Mimbletonia
tono = thunder
Pun = Miltonian
Wordplay = mumble, mimsy/bumble, "M"s
    (keep your annotated *Alice* handy)

* It just so happens that one species of the Mimulus flower has taken a liking to the University of Exeter campus, overgrowning cracks and buildings at an astounding rate. There is also a similar coincidence about one of the leading experts on that species.

—————— *Running Bits* (some tricky ones) ——————

BELLS, RINGS, TONES,
    *"...like **jarring notes** in a familiar **song**..."*
    *"...in a **ringing** voice..."*

HEM, SKIRT
    *"...cleared her throat, '**Hem, hem**,'..."*

PIPES
    *"...**piped** up Neville."*

POKING, CHEST
    *"...**jabbing** himself in the **chest** with a finger."*

STINKING/SMELLS
    *"...the **stinking** Daily Prophet..."*

—————————— *Hints* ——————————

✳ *Items of Intrigue* ✳

DOLORES' PAST There are some *ribbeting* questions about Dolores Umbridge that need to be researched. What secrets is she holding? Did she attend Hogwarts? Once you have been lulled by her dissertation on those subjects, you may want to do some more poking around. Compare those findings with your observations about her relationship with the other teachers – especially her inspection of Professor McGonagall in Chapter 15 {"The Hogwarts High Inquisitor"}.

DOLORES IS A BIT... Check out the mousy-haired Professor Umbridge. Frogs in pink Alice bands is like Snape in Wonderland. You might want to see which of those professors has the worse bite. ✒ *Pink stinks*! ⚡

NEVILLE'S INFORMATION Not everyone thought that Lord Voldything would return. From what Neville said about his feelings on the issue, you should now know of at least one more person who seems to be on our side and was keeping an eagle eye on the situation.

DOUBLE TROUBLE! If you think you're seeing double in Book 5, you should look again. 😊 They are, indeed, clues. Although some relate to the story line, others seem to be growing more prominent. Focus on the alliteration and numerical progressions.

NAME GAME Only a few new students this year. Little tricks with names can give you a new perspective. U should play 2 C if they can B red differently. It's not much harder than trying to visualize budgies on water skis, and it may stop J.K.R. from pulling the wool over your eyes.....

HAT HINTS We've heard the latest hit song from the Sorting Hat. Will it go gold? There were clues, there was foreboding, and there was some more historical information about our patched and frayed (yet hearty) Hat.

It
is
well
to heed
its words;
there's more than
wit inside that Hat.
You'll find wisdom
beyond measure;
plus valuable advice
that you can treasure.
Sing a song of Sorting
The Hat tells what it sees
We admit it has us worried
When what was paired becomes now five...er...three.

The Hat's brain The Sorting Hat is not only good at reading students' minds, but seems to be able to make itself useful in other ways (à la Book 2). Just how useful the Hat will be, may be directly related to how much it knows. What could a dusty thousand-year-old Hat know?

✳ *Secrets and Concealed Clues* ✳

MIMBULUS MIMBLETONIA The WWP Sleuthoscope is testing the limits of our range of awareness...it may be over at the far end of the desk, but it's madly signaling, hoping we get the message (we'll just humor it and go on). Neville's plant isn't just there as window decoration. It does seem to have a function in the septology. Neville likes his plant. Do you like Neville's plant? Are you SURE you like his plant???

UMBRIDGE'S UTTERANCES (We've muffled the HP Hintoscope so you won't hear much out of it.) Professor Umbrage's speech was a mountain of metaphors. You may want to compare it to the BBC interview with J.K.R. {June 19, 2003}, from the week before Book 5 was released. There is something a bit timely in there. You could also check your reading list for information about Assyrian theology. She does have us wondering about her references to those shining examples of the profession who guard the valuable halls of learning.

UMBRIDGE CLUE What's the story behind the shady little toad of a professor? The name, "Umbridge," will give you a little more insight. It is a homophone for another word. The word begins with the same letters so you should be able to find it easily enough. (Once you research it, you may even want to add it to your Running Bits).

✳

Chapter 12 Clues

This is Chapter 12. Think about your list of running bits, and then think doubly.

FAQs

HOW CAN PROFESSOR UMBRIDGE DO THINGS THAT DUMBLEDORE DOESN'T WANT HER TO DO?

That's what everyone is asking, but the reality is that Umbridge truly *does* have the authority. Even though Dumbledore is in charge of the school, he doesn't own it. His situation is no different than any other school headmaster. Dumbledore can make decisions about his staff and students that concern everyday affairs. However, his overall educational plan would have to be approved by the school Board of Governors (you know – the Board that Malfoy used to be on before they booted him out in Book 2). That Board normally appoints or removes the Headmaster, intervenes in crises, and from our experience with Book 5, oversees the OWL and NEWT exams.

From the conversations we have witnessed up through Book 4, there is apparently an ongoing power struggle for control over the school between the Ministry and the Board. They have disagreed on critical issues and have overridden each other in order to implement their own agendas. We have not yet learned how the system is structured, so we don't know what department(s) from the Ministry are involved. In Book 4, Fudge said to Dumbledore "I've given free reign, always." Was he talking as Minister of Magic, or possibly as a member of the Board?

The tricky part, which got very complicated in Book 5, is that somehow (probably the same method that was utilized in Book 2) the Board gave the Ministry enough power to start passing their own rulings. Once the Ministry had that kind of power, they were able to continue issuing whatever decrees they deemed "prudent." That also allowed the Ministry to appoint Umbridge to the position of "High Inquisitor" in Chapter 15 (and we all know how popular that was).

As High Inquisitor, with the legal sanction of the Ministry of Magic behind her, Umbridge was able to do almost anything she thought was necessary – as long as it didn't infringe on Dumbledore's legal authority (of course, as soon as she found that it did, she immediately issued a new decree). Will this major bone of contention between Fudge and Dumbledore, concerning the intervention of the Ministry of Magic into the hallowed halls of learning, be rectified in Book 6?

Running Bits (some tricky ones)

POKING, BUBBLES, SWELLING, CHEST

"*... did not **puncture** the small, hopeful **bubble** that seemed to have **swelled** in his **chest**.*"

SPOTS, CHAIRS
> *"'Poisonous toadstools don't change their spots,'..."*

COLOR (SILVER), MIST
> *"A light silver vapour..."*

Hints

✳ *Items of Intrigue* ✳

Hermione's brain We know Hermione is brainy, but (like Ron said in the first movie) at times she can be *scary*. Chapter 16 {"In the Hog's Head"} has more evidence of her exceptional aptitude. Did you notice that even Harry questions certain things about her brain? HP Sleuths should start thinking about that too.

Evan Snape uses an "Evanesco" spell. The "Evan" part of that word should ring a bell – if not, review the Hints for Chapter 1 {"Dudley Demented"} about a certain 10-year-old. Why is it that anything associated with the word 'Evans' tends to disappear? HP Sleuths might want to check their dictionary to find out. You may also want to question *where* things go when they get vanished...

✳ *Secrets and Concealed Clues* ✳

TT Tutsville Tornadoes are really playing up a storm. The magical world is being caught up in the whirlwind of their victories – wearing the logo on their chest. That logo seems to have a familiar look to it. It sorta reminds us a little of Book 3, an ancient monument, or also one of our running bits. It may have you going in circles if you aren't physically inclined, it's a very simple clue you might just say is as easy as.....

FINGERS AND WANDS In our first Guide, we described the correlation we were seeing between long fingers and magical power. Have HP Sleuths grasped a similar relationship to wands in Book 5?

DREAM DIARY Professor Trelawney has assigned another silly project. She has also (surprise, surprise) assigned us a huge clue.

PEEVES' INFORMATION Have HP Sleuths ever questioned why Peeves is so well-informed? Did you see that he knew quite a bit about Harry? He also had a few wee words of wit that had some familiar notes (think crib).

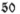

Chapter 13 Clues

HP Sleuths should have the pattern down by now. In every book there is a villain who turns out not to be who we think they are. Yes, it happens in every book – and we've been able to spot the culprit if we read Chapter 13 carefully. Every book... Right?

Did anyone happen to spot the culprit in Book 5?

Was it Kreacher? Causing a death was pretty villainous in our minds. And yet, there wasn't any obvious mention about him in Chapter 13. Maybe it has nothing to do with Sirius and we're barking up the wrong tree. In fact, it just so happens that we do believe we spotted a mention of the real culprit – even nastier than a deranged house-elf. HP Sleuths may want to keep your radar on super-sensitivity and sniff out that rogue.

FAQs

WHAT DO WE NOW KNOW ABOUT THE THIRD TASK FROM BOOK 4?

We now have one of the lingering mysteries from Book 4 cleared up. Hermione explains that no one saw anything that happened in the maze during the third task of the Triwizard Tournament. The audience would have been watching a dark area of bushes while the champions battled for their lives – similar to the way they sat at the edge of the lake during the second task for an hour. Those who have trouble trying to envision what would be so exciting about that probably have the right idea. We can only assume that it was more of a big social gathering than anything else.

CAN HERMIONE REALLY FREE THE HOUSE-ELVES?

It is not like Hermione to get her facts wrong, but then again, she is emotionally tied to her cause. She is also a bit handicapped by a lack of information about it in her favorite history book. Let's see what we know about house-elves and their masters:

A house-elf...

* Is bound to serve one house and one family forever. {Book 2}

* Is considered enslaved; the house-elf's enslavement is tied to the family and all direct descendents. {Book 2 and 5}

* Can only be freed by being "presented" clothes by the master (According to Dobby, the clothing need only be "passed" directly to the house-elf). {Book 2}

* Cannot leave the house (without punishment) unless set free. {Book 5}

* Is bound by the "enchantments of his kind." {Book 5}

⁂ Has extremely powerful magic, but can't use it without permission. {Book 2}

⁂ Keeps the master's secrets, never speaks ill of him, and upholds the family's honor. {Book 4}

⁂ Is never "seen nor heard." {Book 2}

In order to determine if Hermione can free the house-elves with the method she is using, the following questions should be answered:

Is Hermione considered a master?

Since a house-elf is bound to serve a house, they take orders from the whole family who lives there. For instance, Draco would be able to give orders to the family house-elf. As a resident of Hogwarts, it is possible that the students can give orders to the house-elves. As Master, Dumbledore could have given the house-elves an overriding command not to take orders from the students.

How do the students get food from the elves?

When the twins want food, all they have to do is bop on down to the kitchens and put in their request. We've seen Ron place his order for treats, and Dumbledore even reminisced how James used the Invisibility Cloak to nick food from the kitchens. The house-elves are delighted to serve in all cases, so would this be considered taking orders from students or overly-zealous hospitality?

How was Harry able to give Dobby an order?

We see three possible answers to this. One is that Dumbledore *does* allow, or can't stop, all students from issuing orders to the school house-elves; thus, as a resident student, Harry is considered a master. Another is that since Dumbledore knew of the "special circumstances" of Dobby's freedom, he intentionally allowed a loophole for Harry. The third is that, since Dobby is a free elf, he may not be bound by any rules except when given a specific order.

Even though the house-elves wouldn't clean Gryffindor Tower, the only reason Dobby gave was that they were "insulted". Nothing was said regarding fear of being set free; and they are keeping their silence about it. So, if the Hogwarts house-elves pick up one of Hermione's hats by accident, or even on purpose, we still don't know if that would automatically free them. At least we can be sure that Dobby will keep his status as best-dressed house elf. ☺

WHY DOES UMBRIDGE USE THE QUILL WHEN SHE'S GOT FILCH?

It is easy to understand how the black quill would make people think twice about defying Umbridge or one of her rules. What is not as overt is the psychological impact of having the quill engraving into the skin over and over. Umbridge is trying to force her will on people, and those who are less strong in their convictions or less determined to fight, will get the point quickly. However, that quill is a very nasty means of torture. It is more effective than Filch's shackles, especially when attempting to break down those who know they are right and are willing to stand up for their convictions. It is a form of psychological warfare, which fits in very well with the kind of war that Voldemort is fighting right now.

There is an analogy to Umbridge's quill in Franz Kafka's "The Penal Colony" (on your HP Sleuth reading list). If your stomach is up to it, you can read how the "professionals" implement this kind of torture (although even at high school age, it still leaves a mark, so it is **not** recommended for everyone!). Suffice it to say that the deeper it cuts, the deeper the message penetrates. Harry was able to stand up to Umbridge, but if his detention had continued, it is unclear how long he would have endured before being "convinced" not to defy the Queen Toad.

WHY WOULD LUNA BELIEVE IMPOSSIBLE THINGS?
Who only believes in things for which there is no proof? Hermione says that description fits Luna to a "T". As J.K.R. referenced during her appearance in Albert Hall, if you've been in Wonderland, you would also know that the White Queen believed "six impossible things" every morning, because she "practiced." It can be interpreted as Luna having unbridled faith – which allows her to accept concepts that seem impossible. Can that help her to accomplish things that none of the other wizards can? Of course, none of us believe in any of this wizard stuff anyway, do we?

——————*Running Bits* (some tricky ones) ——————

POUNDING, CHAIRS
> *"She **pounded** the arms of her **chair**..."*

MOUTH (OPEN)
> *"...**opened his mouth** to retaliate."*

TWISTED/COILING, WHEEL, STONE
> *"...sitting at the **centre of a knot**..."*
> *"...**stone spiral** staircase..."*
> *"...a few **screwed-up** bits..."*

SINKING, CHAIR
> *"...**sinking** as low in his **chair**..."*
> *"...**so low in his seat** that his nose was roughly level with his **knees**."*

— *Hints* —

✳ *Items of Intrigue* ✳

ONOMATOPOEIA Barking is a running bit, but other animal-type sounds can tell us things too.

HAT CLUES Hats can be made...and Hatters can be mad...but Hermione's flipped her wig on her house-elf clothing factory. You can find a lot of headwear (woolly hats, belled hats, pork pies, etc.) throughout Book 5 (Rule #1); perhaps you can find a thinking cap to help yourself ponder the clues.

SPOTTING NOSES What did Luna have her nose into? If it was a "smudge of earth," at least we know it's not moon dust. Do HP Sleuths recall having seen anyone in Book 1 with spots on them? How about Book 2? Not everyone with spots is a marked person, but it doesn't seem as if life is a prerequisite for having them. Some famous spots appear in *Treasure Island* and *Macbeth*. You may want to bone up about the meaning of "spots" in there.

SNORKACK CLUES What do Crumple-Horned Snorkacks do to get their horns so crumpled? Crumple-Horned Snorkacks may seem odd, but children will recognize the silly sounds of crumpled horns and Snarks from their bedtime rhymes. Unfortunately, Luna's Horn things tell a very sad story that is bound to make you cry. But until HP Sleuths have solved it, you can have fun discovering the tails. A romp through Lewis Carroll and the Kids' Korner of your HP Sleuth reading list will help you hunt this one down. Better hurry before it vanishes...

OLIVER WOOD Did you see Harry's joke about Oliver Wood and Puddlemere United? Are you laughing?

RON AND DIVINATION In this chapter, Ron told Harry he "fancied a walk." What had he told Trelawney?

RON'S PRACTICE How did Ron practice by himself with Quaffles? (Guess all that help from Hermione finally stuck in his brain.)

JUGGLING CLUES The HP Hintoscope is snoring slightly as Harry and Hermione discuss whether Umbridge could be controlled by Voldemort. Why was Harry getting pains? The snoring gets just a bit louder as Harry watches the twins juggle. If you watch the bottles, you may get the idea.... or you may get some needed sleep.

✳ *Secrets and Concealed Clues* ✳

SMALL STUFF, BIG CLUES WWP Sleuthoscope is shrinking away as we try to trap it. We just know this clue is going to get that thing started scurrying around again. We keep seeing some clues about "getting smaller," which seem to relate to the "sinking" running bits. So, HP Sleuths should make sure you start tracking those – you'll probably need at least another couple of feet of parchment.   (hehe)

RUBBISH COLLECTION There's a lot of rubbish being tossed around in Book 5. There are wastebaskets, bins, and just a bunch of talk. HP Sleuths should think like Luna for this one, and go ferreting for the clue. (Hint – it may take you back to Book 4.)

MOONSTONES AND POTIONS What *do* we know about moonstones and their use in potions. Looks like J.K.R. wanted to make sure we're doing our own homework.

SCAR PAIN TRIGGERS The HP Hintoscope is now snorting a bit as it emerges from dozing. When Umbridge touched Harry the first time, he shuddered. The second time, his scar hurt. Did it mean that Umbridge caused the pain? Hermione was doubtful (Rule #4, part a), and we already explained in the first Chapter where *our* minds are regarding the cause of Harry's scar pains. To explain this one, HP Sleuths need to consider covert events going on simultaneously; and beware of big J.K.R. tricks wrapped up inside a little headache.

HARRY'S ANGER Harry doesn't seem to "be himself." Some anger is understandable, but he is always angry. What makes him so mad? Is he in his right mind? Is he in his own mind?

PERMANENT MARKING QUILLS As squeamish as we may get just by thinking about it, a quill like Umbridge's could possibly be used to permanently engrave something crucial into your own skin. HP Sleuths may want to think if anyone may have had something that they thought kneeded to be remembered perfectly. 🖋 *You'd have to be a bit mad, or at least eccentric, to do that to yourself!* ✒

Chapter 14 Clues

(PERCY AND PADFOOT)

FAQs

WHAT DID HARRY'S LETTER TO SIRIUS MEAN?

You'll need your *Philological Stone* to help you here.

Harry wrote in a pseudo-code for his letter to Sirius. It used ambiguities to describe things Harry could not say outright. By doing that, only someone who would have been intimately familiar with the information would have been able to comprehend it. If you had received Harry's letter, this is how you would "read" it:

Harry starts off by telling Sirius, in plain English, that things aren't going very well, so Sirius is prepared to look for clues about what's wrong.

When Harry tells Sirius that Umbridge is "nearly as nice" as his mum, he is saying Umbridge is about *equal in niceness* to Sirius' mother. All Sirius has to do is think about how much he likes his mum, and he knows instantly how much Harry must like Umbridge (blah!). However, someone else who doesn't know Sirius' mum will just assume that Harry is saying that both of them are "nice" (hem-hem).

Then, Harry avoids saying the word he means by saying "that thing I wrote to you about last summer." Although Sirius wrote to Harry at least a couple of times, it seems Harry only wrote to Sirius once. Therefore, it's easy for Sirius to remember that one letter, and to realize Harry is, again, talking about his scar (which no one else would know).

Finally, Harry mentions "our biggest friend," which most people would interpret as a "best" friend. However, the biggest friend they have is *really* big, and with a little thought, Sirius would know from that giant clue it meant "Hagrid."

As with everything we see in J.K.R.'s novels, it's there as a lesson for us. You may want to try out what you learned in other places throughout Book 5 too (wink).

WHY DID FILCH THINK HARRY HAD DUNGBOMBS?

Professor Toad got other people to do her dirty work for her. She also doesn't want to make it obvious that she is trying to intercept legitimate mail from the students (at least not until she has passed an Educational Decree). Her devious method of getting her stubby fingers on Harry's mail with a legal and legitimate excuse entailed telling Filch she suspected Harry of ordering Dungbombs. Filch would not question her source. He would have been quite happy to just confiscate Harry's letter and bring it straight to Umbridge. In that way, Umbridge would have been able to read Harry's mail – even though Dungbombs had never even been on Harry's mind. This is called an "abuse of power" – by which someone in authority twists the rules for their own purposes. Umbridge did a lot of that (which is why we cheered for the Centaurs). Hermione was right to be suspicious.

How Did Umbridge Know Sirius Was In the Fireplace?

In the next chapter {"The Hogwarts High Inquisitor"}, Umbridge says that Marietta's mum works for the Floo Network Office in the Department of Magical Transportation. Umbridge had somehow "recruited" Madam Edgecombe – either willingly or unwillingly – to monitor the school's Floo Network for her. The Floo Network extends beyond the boundaries of the school, so how does this fit in with the security system? We assume that Dumbledore would somehow have some secure way to shut out other flues while still authorizing access to Grimmauld Place. What we don't know is what would have happened if Umbridge caught hold of Sirius' head.

———— *Running Bits* (some tricky ones) ————

Turns (left, right)
    *"...instead of **turning right**, he **turned left**..."*

Mouth (open), 2s
    *"...**opened his mouth** furiously, **mouthed** for a few **seconds**..."*

Ears, Rings, Tones
    *"...still **ringing** in his **ears**."*
    *"...making a right **pig's ear**..."*

———————— *Hints* ————————

✳ *Items of Intrigue* ✳

Weird news There was a slightly *Weird* piece of information that Hermione saw in the newspaper, which we also found interesting.

Paracelsus Paracelsus was a bit strange. If you do your Rowlinguistics research, you may conclude that he was probably a Slytherin. We've never encountered this strange guy before, have we? ♟ *Don't go jumping to conclusions – think Book 1... think chocolate...*

De Umbridge Sirius offers his opinion on whether or not Umbridge is a Death Eater. Even if she is not, would that stop her from doing something horrible and *illegal*? Check Chapter 32 {"Out of the Fire"} if you want help on this.

SCRATCHING FOR CLUES Filch's eyes did a "raking" action on Harry. The Bowtruckles clawed him. Even Draco scratched at the back of Harry's neck in the Quidditch match. People and creatures in Book 5 have their talons out, don't they? We recommend that HP Sleuths do some digging into these clues.

✳ Secrets and Concealed Clues ✳

WRIGGLING CLUES The WWP Sleuthoscope is squirming in anguish (we'll just act like we didn't notice). The Slytherins are doing it again – more nasty insults to the Gryffindor team. And more detective work for HP Sleuths seeking clues.

SYMBOLS There is a running bit (think flywheel) that is very cleverly hidden in this chapter. It parallels other (just as subtle) references, which should be turning the wheels in your brain: Check the imagery here of Harry's visit to the Owlery against the bicycles in Chapter 1 {"Dudley Demented'}, the egg cups in Chapter 31 {"OWLs"}, and the swiveling staircases in Chapter 32 {"Out of the Fire"}. A link to all these can be found in a symbol relating to a Celtic/Druid god.

STURGIS CLUES The details about Sturgis Podmore and the break-in should be scrutinized for clues and should be compared (time-wise) to another painful event back in the previous chapter. The town he comes from might be friendly, but the foliage certainly is not. Reminds us of the house in the W. W. Jacobs story from your HP Sleuth reading list.

PERCY'S LETTER The WWP Sleuthoscope is quivering from nervousness and there is a trail of ink snaking out of it. How carefully did Ron read Percy's letter? How carefully did *you* read it? You may want to try out your previous lesson from this chapter. Think about Harry's letter to Sirius. Make sure you've got your *Philological Stone* handy. We spotted a number of coincidental references that have started us quivering, as well. How about:

> ✳ The escape of ten (yes, 10) Azkaban prisoners
>
> ✳ The whereabouts of a certain ratfink
>
> ✳ Info about our first Prisoner of War!

Now you can search for those along with all the other clues. While you're doing so, think about why all those clues would be in there...

---- ✳ ----

Chapter 15 Clues

FAQs

WHY IS CONJURING MORE DIFFICULT THAN VANISHING?

If you want to pass your Transfiguration NEWTs, this may help. There are six degrees of difficulty given for vanishing and conjuring:

Least difficult .... to .... **Most difficult**

Vanishing ———————————————	Conjuring ———————————————
inanimate invertebrate vertebrate	inanimate invertebrate vertebrate

*Just to clarify things: An "**inanimate**" object is something non-living so it isn't very animated (doesn't tend to move around much). A "**vertebrate**" is a creature with a (internal) skeleton – having a backbone with vertebrae, such as a raven or human, which is typically more intelligent. An "**invertebrate**" is usually low intelligence with no bones – something slimy and squishy like a worm or (you guessed it) a slug.*

The magic in J.K.R.'s world seems to take into account the complexity of the object or creature to which it is being directed. The more complex the object or creature, the more difficult it is to perform magic on it. The degree to which it has the "essence of life" and "free will" makes a difference. That means that while Vanishing a hat is a no-brainer, a lion would take a *lot* more skill (especially when it's charging!).

CAN WIZARDS REPAIR ANYTHING?

Magic can do very cool things. We have already seen it fix broken bones, allow people to fly, and even make things disappear (we're still working on Draco). However, magic also has limits. It cannot bring back the dead, and it can only fix things – not create or recreate them. In our first Guide, we explained how conjuring "out of thin air" is a temporary condition – as described by J.K.R. in her interview with SouthwestNews.com (July, 2000). The conjured object only lasts for a short time (although we still don't know how long is "short" or what determines the timeframe).

Repairing objects, however, is possible and is done routinely. But we now know there are even limits to that kind of magic. When Harry knocked over his bowl of Murtlap, that was yet another lesson for us. It taught us that even though we can fix a container with "Reparo!", we can't put the essence back into it. The container can be repaired, but the spilled contents are lost (unless what was in there was owl treats – bet Pig would find those!).

We see the same circumstances in *Professor* Snape's office in Chapter 26 {"Seen and Unforseen"}, where the liquid encasing an oogie leaked out of the broken jar. Although *Professor* Snape repaired the jar, the liquid that had already escaped ended up on Harry's robe (uck!).

Ultimately, these lessons were to reinforce the sad fact that once the prophecy orbs were smashed, the contents could never be "repaired" or retrieved. ☹

——————— *Running Bits* (some tricky ones) ———————

MOON STUFF
*"...an exciting **new phase...**"*

BELLS, RINGS, TONES
*"...**bangles clinking.**"*

CORNERS
*"She **cornered** him..."*

——————————— *Hints* ———————————

✴ *Items of Intrigue* ✴

MARCHBANKS AND OGDEN CLUES   Griselda Marchbanks and Tiberius Ogden resigned from the Wizengamot to protest the appointment of an Inquisitor (don't do that – we need you!). We know that when characters are mentioned more than once, that we should be taking good notes and a closer look at them. We later see Marchbanks in Chapter 31 {"OWLs"}, where we learn some interesting details about her and her circle of acquaintances. Her name etymology raises several questions – not to mention it is a concatenation of two running bits. We aren't sure if we have seen Tiberius before or not, since only the last name is familiar (it was a favorite of Gilderoy's in Book 2, and a few others since). Tiberius' name seems to have Greek and Middle East origins with some very interesting mythologies (check your mythology reading list). He may also have a thriving business in the beverage industry.

WE DON'T MISS IT BUT...   We haven't seen a lot of Binns' class in Book 5, but have you been paying attention to the goblin mentions sneaking around? Instead, Binns has been covering one very big important subject. According to the hints in Book 5, Binns seems to have an important name too (at least for Sleuth scavengers).

SNAPE'S HANDWRITING   Check out Snape's handwriting – at least the "D" he put on Harry's essay. Anime and TV serial buffs may be particularly interested in that "D," while others can just ponder the symbolism in the *lines* of it. The debate soars on. Don't ever think J.K.R. isn't playing with us.....

TRELAWNEY'S ANCESTOR   Trelawney's ancestor is said to have been a celebrated seer. But if we go by her name, her great-great-grandmother may have had some problems with her predictions as well (check your mythology reading list). We keep wondering about Sybill's future.

SMASHED MURTLAP   The Murtlap incident should make HP Sleuths think young. You can revert back (or check your crib notes) to see a running bit or two (or more) hidden in that scene.

Hermione gave Harry a bowl of Murtlap to soak,
but when he got mad it fell over and broke.
All of the spells known to all the best men,
couldn't put the Murtlap back in there again.

BEHOLD! THE HIGH INQUISITOR The High Inquisitor title may have a familiar tone for classical music enthusiasts. If a certain hit song from the Mikado is running around in your head, then you would have had no doubt what the toad lady is up to. You may also think Luna-style about the characters and plot in there. (Those less classically-inclined can do a lookup in your supplies list).

CRUPS What have HP Sleuths learned about Crups, Porlocks, Knarls, and Bowtruckles? Crups were mentioned more than once – their similarity to a certain Muggle animal should make you think of bits of tableware and kid stuff (check *Fantastic Beasts* and your crib notes).

✳ *Secrets and Concealed Clues* ✳

STONY CLUES The WWP Sleuthoscope is slowly turning at the cusp of the desk...we don't care, because our attention is on this monumental clue! HP Sleuths in the UK probably caught the reference, but those in the U.S. should look up Lucius Malfoy's address to see what wizard-like artifacts may be just a stone's throw from his manor. As with all hints in Book 5, there are several meanings stacked into this clue (several month's worth of them).

VENOM More venom antidotes. Mr. Weasley sure needed one for his non-healing venom injury. You know what Imposter Moody said about such things... CONSTANT VIGILANCE!

GRUESOME DEATH Professor Trelawney was up to her tricks again, so hopefully HP Sleuths were awake for this class! She had "foretold a gruesome and early death." If you use your *Philological Stone*, you will see that not only did someone die, but she was giving us a big clue — which will be a bigger clue by Book 6!

MINISTRY INSIDER Someone from the Ministry was quoted in an article from the *Daily Prophet* – about Umbridge's appointment as High Inquisitor. That "someone" isn't on our side. Who was it? There could be a hint if you read closely what was said about "reposing confidence." It could be a stretch, but we have seen that "repose" word used in conjunction with a certain social environment of Henry David Thoreau. What do HP Sleuths think?

COMBING FOR CLUES Harry, Ron, and Hermione are combing through the Daily Prophet for information. We hope that HP Sleuths are following their example to the letter...

Chapter 16 Clues

FAQs

WHO WAS THE BANDAGED MAN IN THE HOG'S HEAD?
See next question for the answer...

WHO WAS RESPONSIBLE FOR THE REGURGITATING TOILETS?
See next question for the answer...

WHO WAS THE CULPRIT BEHIND THE BITING DOORKNOBS?
Haven't you now figured out the answer? The Muggle-baiting mysteries were cleared up by Mr. Weasley in Chapter 22 {"St Mungo's Hospital for Magical Maladies and Injuries} when he discussed an article about the arrest of Willy Widdershins. It seems that Willy was responsible for both the regurgitating toilets and the biting doorknobs. Professor Umbridge then confirmed that Willy was also the bandaged man in the Hog's Head. He had been her informant, ratting on the students' off-grounds meeting. Yes, Willy Widdershins was a very busy man. In fact, we believe he was involved in yet one more deal, but we have no proof except Rule #3 (see our Hints for Chapter 5 {"Order of the Phoenix"}). Did you wonder why Willy was all bandaged? Remember – he got injured when his toilet spell backfired on him (pew!). Guess he didn't quit while he was ahead.

What Students Were In Dumbledore's Army?

MEMBERS OF THE D.A.

Hannah Abbot *(H)*	Justin Finch-Fletchley *(H)*	Padma Patil *(R)*
Katie Bell *(G)*	Seamus Finnigan* *(G)*	Parvati Patil *(G)*
Susan Bones *(H)*	Anthony Goldstein *(R)*	Harry Potter *(G)*
Terry Boot *(R)*	Hermione Granger *(G)*	Zacharias Smith *(H)*
Lavender Brown *(G)*	Angelina Johnson *(G)*	Alicia Spinnet *(G)*
Cho Chang *(R)*	Lee Jordan *(G)*	Dean Thomas *(G)*
Michael Corner *(R)*	Neville Longbottom *(G)*	Fred Weasley *(G)*
Colin Creevey *(G)*	Luna Lovegood *(R)*	George Weasley *(G)*
Dennis Creevey *(G)*	Ernie Macmillan *(H)*	Ginny Weasley *(G)*
Marietta Edgecombe *(R)*		Ron Weasley *(G)*

Note: Seamus Finnegan attended only the last meeting

———— *Running Bits* (some tricky ones) ————

TAILS
> *"...they **queued** up..."*
> *"...long **plait** down her back..."*

STUBBY
> *"...the **stubs** of candles..."*

FREEZING
> *"...**frozen** in the act..."*

———————— *Hints* ————————

✳ *Items of Intrigue* ✳

LOVE TRIANGLE Hermione is still communicating with Krum, and Ron is still very jealous. If any HP Sleuth thinks that "Vicky" could ever go out with Hermione, then you also had better be assuming that Ron's not around to see it....

LIL' SIS Who does Ron want Ginny to go out with? If you are having trouble answering that, you may want to reread Ron's harried comments to Hermione on the subject.

CAT AND MICE Now let's see... we have three vanished mice...three vanished mice. And one vanishing kitty (no mention of a smile). HP Sleuths should know these strange sights, but if you need help, Kid's Korner and Wonderland will provide. However, don't get distracted by fairy tales when there's a mouse-tail on the loose....

HOG'S MEETING The purpose of the student meeting, along with the title of this chapter may conjure images of certain animal farms (look up George Orwell on your reading list). There are several analogies that not only work in Book 5, but may need to be heeded as the War evolves.

CHEWY CLUES You can really sink your teeth into all the clues in Book 5. Literally. Did you see the chewing and chomping? Must have something to do with teeth, wouldn't you say?

✳ *Secrets and Concealed Clues* ✳

THE HOG'S HEAD The WWP Sleuthoscope is making inappropriate motions to get our attention! Starting with the Hog's Head sign displaying the ghastly head of the decapitated boar, there are several clues lurking in the corners of this "fine establishment." The Hog's Head smells like a goat, the bartender has a beard like a goat... Do we know any goats? Harry did think the bartender looked familiar. HP Sleuths may want to sniff for clues – especially in Chapter 24 {"Rita Skeeter's Scoop"} of Book 4.

FLITWICK'S WARNING Hermione verified with Professor Flitwick that students are allowed to go to the Hog's Head, but he warned to not use the glasses there. Which part of that information seems the strangest to you? (Hint – NEWT-level question)

CORNERS Ginny's little Michael sat in a corner, just to tease HP Sleuths. And now J.K.R. has given us links, which your reading list helps to deduce. What's going on in the corners? You should check to make sure there's no hanky-panky. (Your Kids' Korner crib notes is one place to look.)

WILLY WIDDERSHINS CLUES All you need for this one are your dictionaries (both UK and U.S.), your list of running bits, your *Philological Stone*, and about 24 hours of nothing but following the leads for all the definitions of his names!

Chapter 17 Clues

FAQs

Does Snape Really Want to Teach Defense Against the Dark Arts?

Rumor has it that Snape really wants the job of Defense Against the Dark Arts, but Dumbledore won't give it to him. We can be reasonably sure from Umbridge's inspection of Snape's class that the rumors are, indeed, correct. Snape confirmed he has applied for the position every year and has yet to be appointed. So, why does Dumbledore refuse to appoint him? Dumbledore may have reasons similar to Jedi Master Yoda's criteria for students. Then again, it could be like keeping a drink away form a recovering alcoholic (Avada Kedavras Anonymous)?

Why is Umbridge Inspecting the Teachers?

Umbridge is an evil person, but she didn't conduct those inspections just to be mean. There were several strategies she had in mind – all of which coincidentally (hem-hem) were a benefit to Voldemort and his plans. Her primary reasons for "inspecting" the teachers seem to have been:

- Discerning teacher allegiances – who is for/against Dumbledore
- Controlling the curriculum at Hogwarts so that students are unable to defend themselves
- Using her Inquisitorial Squad as intimidation and for spying on those who were aware of Voldemort's return
- Determining what teacher would be easiest and least controversial to sack
- Removing teachers who would present the biggest barriers to her plans (or to anyone else who could be thinking of infiltrating the school)
- Discrediting Dumbledore through his choice of faculty
- Convincing the Ministry that Dumbledore is incompetent overall in his methods of running the school
- Possibly covering for her desire to remove Trelawney from the protection of Hogwarts (remember — Umbridge told Filch to look for Dungbombs when she was really spying on Harry)

It just doesn't seem as if all of these would benefit the Ministry or Fudge (in fact, you might argue that removing Trelawney would improve the reputation of the school). Was Umbridge doing this because she knew what Voldemort needed, or does she just see things from the same perspective?

——————— *Running Bits* (some tricky ones) ———————

TWISTED, COILING
 *"...**curly** signature..."*

WHEELS, FALLING BACK
 *"...arms working madly **like windmills**, then he **toppled over backwards**..."*

BELLS, RINGS, TONE
 *"...in a **high-pitched** voice..."*
 *"...old-fashioned **rings**..."*

————————————— *Hints* —————————————

✳ *Items of Intrigue* ✳

INSPECTING BINNS Why would Umbridge not inspect the deadly boring Professor Binns? HP Sleuths should think about her intentions, and consider what she may or may not be able to do to him. Queen Toad may consider Binns and his lessons to be rubbish, but HP Sleuths know that "one man's garbage is another man's treasures." 😊

SLIP OF THE TONGUE What did Professor Binns call Harry? Did you hear that? We know he's not very much in touch with reality, but that has a touch of Rule #3.

BANNED FROM THE HOG'S HEAD No one will argue that Mundungus Fletcher isn't the most upstanding member of the magical community. How bad can he be? What evidence do you need? Why was he banned? When did that happen? Knowing J.K.R., you may want to cross-reference any events that happened around that time.

GRUBBLY-PLANK CLUES Grubbly-Plank has a familiar sound to it (the kind Luna would like to read about). HP Sleuths should think about this one from a metonymy perspective. If you are clever, something will hit you in the head – which will then hopefully help you solve the very next question here. Such as... where Dumbledore finds a substitute teacher in a pinch (who just happens to know about magical beasts)? And what kind of female smokes a pipe? You can sniff out some clues about this if you revisit the Leaky Cauldron in Book 1.

WILHELMINA CLUES Wilhelmina is a feminine version of the German name, "Wilhelm." That brings you right back to an old grimm clue.

✳ Secrets and Concealed Clues ✳

POMEGRANATE Snape can cause Neville to melt his cauldrons six times, and even Harry must have messed up his potions at least that many times by now. Harry wasn't supposed to be adding pomegranate *anything* (not even one seed) to his Strengthening Solution. Those HP Sleuths who are up on their mythology will know that even a little pomegranate is too much pomegranate. (You end up in places that can really be a downer.)

HARRY'S TAIL According to Sirius, Harry was being tailed by the Order even when he visited Hogsmeade. HP Sleuths should think about who is doing the surveillance and how.

RON'S WORDS Ron quipped, *"Are you serious? Ah, Hermione, you're a life-saver..."* If you were expecting us to comment further on this, then you must be new around here... ☺

✳

Chapter 18 Clues

(DUMBLEDORE'S ARMY)

─────────────── *FAQs* ───────────────

Why Did WWP Miss the Hint About the Chamber Pot Room?

As most HP Sleuths now know, our *Ultimate Unofficial Guide* theories were correct concerning almost all of the mysteries revealed *so far....* except for one obvious "oop!" where we rejected the Chamber Pot Room as a candidate for the "Room of Requirement." Yes — we were fooled. You see, J.K.R. tricked us (and we fell for it!). Geesh.

And this is why we blew it... We verrrry carefully read the exact quote from the interview where she revealed that there would be a magical Room (*BBC Online*, March 12, 2001). This is how J.K.R. described the room:

"...a...room, mentioned in book four, which has certain magical properties Harry hasn't discovered yet!"

The criteria we used for speculating which room it would be was solely from that quote. These comprised the basis for our conclusion:

1. It was described as a room
2. It was mentioned in Book 4
3. The room, itself, has magical properties
4. Harry hadn't yet discovered the magical properties
5. Since Harry hadn't **yet** figured out the magical properties, that implied he had been in the room **already**, but just hadn't discovered those properties

As we now know, it was, indeed, the Chamber Pot room that was the Room of Requirement in Book 5. Although we had considered the Chamber Pot room, we immediately rejected it — based on the last item in that list. You see, we knew Harry had never been in Dumbledore's Chamber Pot room. (Groan)

So, we either should have considered that the *room* – as well as its magical properties – hadn't been discovered by Harry, or (see Hints section below).

How Did Harry Get Back the Marauder's Map?

When last we knew...

In Chapter 25 {"The Egg and the Eye"} of Book 4, Imposter Moody had narrowly saved Harry from Filch, Snape, and nosy Mrs. Norris – as Harry huddled under the Invisibility Cloak with his leg stuck in the trick stair. During that ordeal, Imposter Moody had spotted Harry's map sitting on a step and retrieved it just in time to prevent Snape from nabbing it. Once Harry was free, Imposter Moody (who marveled at the map), asked to borrow it – which Harry thought was fair repayment (not knowing, of course, how it would be used). At the end of Book 4, Imposter Moody still had the map somewhere in his possession at the time that he was kissed by the Dementor, so we had questioned where that map was going to end up in Book 5. As it turns out, Harry did get it back. We're not sure if he retrieved it himself, or it was given back to him. That is the interesting question.

———————— *Running Bits* (some tricky ones) ————————

SHARP/EDGES, EGG
   *"'...he's **keen** to kind of . . . **egg** us on.'"*

JUMPING
   *"...a strange **leaping** feeling..."*

SLIDING, HAND
   *"...**slipped** from Harry's **slack grip**..."*

———————————— *Hints* ————————————

✳ *Items of Intrigue* ✳

STUDENT BACKGROUNDS Throughout Book 5, Harry's classmates divulged some interesting tidbits about their relatives. We hope HP Sleuths have started a dossier scroll on each.

BLACKBIRDS Fans of classic horror literature will have immediately recognized J.K.R.'s satirical sense of humor as Harry, Ron, and Hermione sit at their writing desk, trying to silence a raven. You can search the works of Lewis Carroll and Edgar Allan Poe for yet more pesky blackbirds. A timely tapping at their chamber door will find you spellbound forever more.

TALL TEMPER Although Harry didn't know where Voldemort was, from the description of Voldemort's temper, Harry did know it was mounting. Have you noticed that Voldemort's temper isn't the only thing getting bigger in book 5? HP Sleuths should be making notes in your mounting tower of parchment.

HAMMERING RAIN The weather is as miserable as Harry's year at school. With all the hammering and pounding that the rain is doing, you'd think something was going up – not coming down....

✳ *Secrets and Concealed Clues* ✳

RECONSIDERING THE ROOM If J.K.R. truly was precise with the wording of her Room of Requirement hint, she may *still* be fooling us! If she was stating that Harry had already been in Room of Requirement before, that opens several other mesmerizing possibilities. Could he have already been in that room? We don't want to lead you astray again, so only those HP Sleuths who share our suspicions should investigate this. If you reflect on some scenes from Book 1, when Harry might have desperately been seeking a room, it does make sense. Our Rememberit Quill has scrawled ~ *We can't be sure what floors Harry was on then, so don't go giving anyone a hard time about that.*

MARIETTA CLUES Not only do we dislike Cho's friend, we don't trust someone called Marietta Edgecombe. It reminds us of some hairy experiences Harry had a while ago. *Stop wattling around, and think for a second.*

SWELLING Harry's done it once again. He lost control just a bit and swelled his frog ("blowups happen"). By now HP Sleuths should be getting the idea that, just like in Book 3, there is something major to this getting bigger thing.

GRIMMAULD PLACE Grimmauld Place assuredly does not have a positive effect on people. HP Sleuths may want to look a little closer at how worried Hermione has been about Sirius being cooped up in that wretched house.

SUPPLIES The WWP Sleuthoscope is shaking so hard from all the pent-up excitement that we had to stop it from spinning off the desk and cracking (we don't want to have to make a trip to Dervish & Banges). Where does the Room of Requirement obtain the supplies that are required? HP Sleuths who read carefully will be able to draw certain conclusions about that. Those who read *very* carefully could notice some glaring discrepancies!

SECRET WEAPON Harry had been trying to imagine where Voldemort was keeping his secret weapon when Ron interrupted him. You may think that is a storyline clue, but WWP counts it as a secret septology clue.

DREAMING OF CORRIDORS Harry falls asleep, his book falls to the floor, and he falls into a dream of a windowless corridor, with a door at the end. Now that you have finished Book 5, HP Sleuths know exactly what this door dream was hinting at, right?

Chapter 19 Clues

(The Lion and the Serpent)

FAQs

Why Doesn't Harry Question Things More?

When Harry has wondered about his parents, his family, or other things in his background, why hasn't he asked someone about it? When Umbridge was torturing him, why didn't he discuss it with one of the other teachers? When Harry thought that the reason Dumbledore wasn't looking at him was because he was angry at him, why didn't Harry ask what was going on?

We have only one response – don't ask questions! (The Dursleys *do* get their point across.)

Running Bits (some tricky ones)

Toilets
"Hey, Potty..."

Hands
"Get a grip..."

Spots
"...snow-flecked window..."

Spindly, Trunk
"Derrick and Bole..."

Hints

✳ Items of Intrigue ✳

Talisman The HP Hintoscope is just barely humming a little love song under its breath. Harry feels as if he has a talisman in his chest. Astute HP Sleuths will realize that was not just a metaphor. What could it be? We're assuming it was what saved him in Chapter 36 {"The Only One He Ever Feared"}.

Lion hat Luna's magic, such as her wild lion hat, is not just loony stuff. We hope HP Sleuths noted the effect of Luna's ludicrous lion roar.

Montague clues The name "Montague" should remind HP Sleuths of a tragic love affair from Shakespeare. It is also has a tie to Aunt Marge's dog, which wouldn't be the only reference in Book 5. When we hear the name of her dog, we now think of Nursery Rhymes (somehow, we don't think that's what Marge had in mind.)

✳ Secrets and Concealed Clues ✳

MAGICAL MARKS Hermione's Protean Charm worked very similarly to how the Death Eater mark works. There seem to be many ways of "marking" people, and since we are aware that wizard-type marks can have special links and powers, Hermione's comments on the issue should raise questions about all kinds of marks.

LIONS AND SERPENTS (OH MY!) The WWP Sleuthoscope is emitting a low growl. Lions and serpents don't usually mix. In fact, Hogwarts is a perfect example of that. However, Newt Scamander has found one instance in which they do. We highly recommend that HP Sleuths start tracking it in your well-trampled copy of *Fantastic Beasts*.

Chapter 20 Clues

FAQs

Did We Learn Anything New About How the Marauder's Map Works?

The answer is "no" (drat!). We did see another ghost go by (Nick) with the map right there in Harry's hand, but Harry didn't mention if he even saw a nearly-dot on there. Therefore, we still don't know if ghosts show up on the map or not.

In Book 5, Harry had to keep the map well-hidden from Umbridge and her spies, so he rarely pulled it out to look at it. In fact, in all books, when Harry did look at the map, he was in a hurry and only checked it for threatening activity. He was not likely to notice someone like Pettigrew back in his dorm among all those other dots, when he was worried about the ones much nearer to him. That is probably the way it was used by Fred and George, and they had already memorized it. Since the map is both illegal and valuable, it is not very likely that any of the kids had it out and studied it for very long. If the map works as we have speculated in our first Guide and it only shows those who are moving, then not everyone would show up anyway – especially if they were seated or curled up in bed. That means there may have been other undesirable entities lurking around Hogwarts in Book 5, but Harry would not have known from the map.

Running Bits (some tricky ones)

Spindly, Poking/Sharp, Mouth
 "...steak out of Fang's mouth."

Muffled, silence
 "...a stifled noise..."

Circles/Round/Wheels
 "Umbridge wheeled round...

Hints

✳ *Items of Intrigue* ✳

Finding giants You wouldn't think that it would be difficult to find a bunch of twenty-foot giants, but they were supposed to have been very-well-hidden twenty-foot giants. Did Hagrid have any trouble finding them? Have HP Sleuths *carefully* thought about why someone would have been so well-informed?

Avoiding magic Hagrid explained that he and Mme Maxime had to avoid using magic once they got near the giants because Death Eaters could have been around. Think about what that implies.

HAGRID'S TALE Get out your *Philological Stone* to reveal the double-entendre in the title of this chapter. Hagrid describes how someone was pursuing him and Mme Maxime on their way to the giants, but they lost him in France. Did HP Sleuths spy who sent him, or consider how anyone could lose sight of two half-giants?

GIANT PRESENTS Humans giving presents of fire to giants is another clever J.K.R. parody (and, of course, a clue). If you wanna get the joke, you can look up Prometheus in your mythology references.

PUNNY Here's a quiz: *Kreacher* is to *creature*.... as *Karkus* is to _____ . (With a name like that, we should have known he'd be dead meat.)

FLYING MYSTERIES Hagrid flew to get to Harry at the shack in Book 1, but he doesn't like brooms. So what else would he have used? That little mystery may have been solved in Book 5. Similarly, Dumbledore flew to London in record time Book 1. Now that had to have been a funny sight.

FANGS Fang the fearless boarhound isn't the only fang hanging around. There's a fair number of strange fanged things in Book 5 that really shouldn't need tooth-brushes. That many fangs in a J.K.R. story cannot mean anything good.

SHARP WIT Have HP Sleuths been staying on top of all the running bits? We're not sure what all the spindles and pokey objects are for. Unless...naw...there would-n't be a need for a vampire hunter, would there?

✳ *Secrets and Concealed Clues* ✳

GOLGOMATH CLUES You may need to use your Philological Stone on this one. The name of the giant, Golgomath, has a close resemblance to a very famous mytho-logical hero from Mesopotamia. That hero, was only part god, had adventures and a quest that give us many big clues about Book 5.

INSIDE INFORMATION Who knew the whereabouts of Hagrid and Mme Maxime? Who else seemed to know in this chapter? You should think verrrry carefully about who should have known what information and if there was a contradiction in there.

PRESENT OF A CLUE Another of the giant presents has a long history in legend and fantasy. Indestructible armour from goblins and other magical critters can be also be found in works by J.R.R. Tolkien and Philip Pullman (on your reading list). Don't forget that a helmet is just a very sturdy hat.

✳

Chapter 21 Clues

FAQs

You may or may not have noticed, but there are a trunkful of running bits and clues that all relate back to Mad-Eye Moody and/or his nemesis, Imposter Moody. Did you see all the one-eyes or one-eye-bigger references? How about damaged legs, noses, and lopsided things? In this chapter, we see *"gnarled," "Mazin,"* and *"lopsided ...I'm not mad!"* (jux-ta-position). Something's afoot.

Here is where you should start looking. Take your list of running bits and go back to Book 4. Look at the passage describing Mad-Eye Moody's entrance when we first met him in Chapter 12 {"The Triwizard Tournament"} of Book 4. You will encounter approximately 30 Book 5 running bits in the description of his big entrance – in addition to several "coincidentally" prominent phrases used in Book 5. Check your Dark Detectors carefully as you read:

U.S.: pages 184 – 185
UK: pages 163 – 164

We know that Moody is back again for Book 5, but we don't see much of him. Therefore, all these Moody clues should have caught the eye of HP Sleuths and gotten you started searching for the instigator. Why are these hints here? Probably because they are the keys to the secrets in Book 5? We've already shown you all this, but we will give you one more hint to help you solve it.... Think Trick-or-Treat. Think *analogy.* Think...

CONSTANT VIGILANCE!

Running Bits (some tricky ones)

STAMP, MARCH, TREE
   "...stumping out of the forest..."

TREE, HEADS
   "...often at loggerheads."

HOT/COLD
   "...sweating and shivering feverishly."

CEILING (HOMOPHONE)
   "...sealing it..."

Hints

✳ Items of Intrigue ✳

SEEING THESTRALS There were three people who could see the Thestrals: Harry, Neville and Rule #2. Did HP Sleuths get a good look at him at least?

UMBRIDGE AND THESTRALS Was Umbridge able to see Thestrals? Have you got your rules handy?

✳ Secrets and Concealed Clues ✳

BEING ALERT Did anyone happen to notice who went for Professor McGonagall when Harry woke from his vision of the attack on Mr. Weasley? That was quick thinking, wasn't it?

CHIMAERA The WWP Sleuthoscope is shuffling stealthily along the edge of the desk...thinking that it can pretend to not be there. But we're going to ignore it for now. Harry, Ron, and Hermione were worried that Hagrid might have had a Chimaera (look it up in *Fantastic Beasts* if you don't remember those). Hermione mentions how no one "in their right mind" would be interested in Knarls over Chimaeras. She is sure (Rule #4a) that Hagrid doesn't have one – as she seems to have discussed the availability of their eggs with him already. However, HP Sleuths may still want to think very hard about that discussion and not make assumptions.

THE SNAKE The WWP Sleuthoscope just slithered to the middle of the desk (thinks it's being coy). What kind of snake attacked Mr. Weasley? What did the snake do? What did it *not* do? Was it Nagini? It was confirmed in the first chapter of Book 4 that Nagini is venomous. Her name etymology tells us that she could have a relationship to a Nag duo in your Rudyard Kipling reading).

WHO DONE IT Harry walked into the Come and Go Room to find that someone had hung a hundred ornaments – each with an image of his face on it. He had just pulled them all down before the first member of the DA arrived (Luna). Do HP Sleuths note anything suspicious? Do you want to check a couple of your Rules of Constant Vigilance?

GLASSES The WWP Sleuthoscope is making bugeyes at us, and threatening to start into a tie-raid! Except for the beginning of Book 1, where Dudley was "designing" Harry's eyewear, people's eyeglasses are not referenced very often. In fact, we can sometimes forget that Professor McGonagall, Dumbledore, Mr. Weasley, and Percy all wear glasses. However, in Book 5, we are constantly reminded of eyewear. This big clue is intended to make sure we don't lose sight of a certain person. HP Sleuths should be aware that this is one of the focal points of Book 5. If you can see this clue, everything else becomes much clearer.

Chapter 22 Clues

FAQs

WHAT IS BUTTERBEER – CAN IT MAKE YOU DRUNK?

The students are permitted to drink butterbeer and we haven't seen any of them get drunk on it. Yet, Winky got totally stewed. Is it alcoholic or not? In Chapter 28 of Book 4 {"The Madness of Mr. Crouch"}, Harry implies that there is certainly some alcohol or alcohol-type substance in butterbeer, *"...it's not strong, that stuff."* But Dobby answers, *"Tis strong for a house-elf."* So, we know that there is, indeed, a form of alcoholic ingredient in butterbeer, but it's not very effective on a human (although we haven't tried it on Professor Flitwick yet). ☺

IS THERE A CURE FOR LYCANTHROPY (WEREWOLFISM)?

Madam Pomfrey can cure broken bones in less than an hour and even re-grow them overnight. It is evident that wizard healers have capabilities far beyond Muggle doctors. Additionally, just like in Muggle medicine, wizard medical researchers also make new discoveries. For instance, even though it's not a cure, we learned in Book 3 about "Wolfsbane Potion," which can make a werewolf docile. And that had not even been discovered when Lupin was a kid. Nonetheless, according to Mr. Weasley in Chapter 22 {"St Mungo's Hospital for Magical Maladies and Injuries"}, there is no cure.

In Book 2, however, Gilderoy Lockhart boasted that he had completely cured a werewolf with the *"immensely complex Homorphus Charm."* Even though he was a big fake and didn't personally do any of his feats, they were supposed to have been based on events that *really happened.* He bragged how he cunningly extracted the details of how a wizard accomplished his amazing spell, and then zap the poor guy's memory. As he was already a liar, maybe the story of curing a werewolf was just a tall tufted tale. However, we have to wonder if, through greed and petty self-indulgence, Gilderoy may have destroyed the mind of a person who had discovered a cure for all the people who suffer as Lupin does.

So, do wizards currently know of a cure? The answer is "no." Is there really a cure? Only "Mr. Smiley" knew for sure... and lately he's not much help (less than usual, even...).

WHAT IS DUMBLEDORE'S WIDGET, AND WHAT DID IT TELL HIM?

Are you aware that we may have seen Dumbledore's delicate silver instrument previously? In Chapter 5 {"Diagon Alley"} of Book 1, Harry sees some *"strange silver instruments"* in the shops at Diagon Alley. The description isn't detailed enough, so we can't be sure, but Rule #3 tells us that we should mention it or we're not doing our job.

As Dumbledore said, in Chapter 37 {"The Lost Prophecy"}, he had suspected the powers of that scar all along. Nonetheless, it wasn't until Harry witnessed/participated in the attack on Mr. Weasley, that Dumbledore was able to verify it.

Dumbledore's little instrument seemed to be able to tap into the underlying cause of Harry's mental and physical state. It sort of reminded us of reading smoke signals or Firenze's description of reading fumes from burning sage and mallowsweet. Just like smoke signals, it began with little puffs that kept getting longer and longer until they connected into long spiraling plumes of smoke. Then, suddenly the one plume divided (cell-like) into two identical plumes.

This is what provided Dumbledore's observation that Harry's predicament had something to do with being *"...in essence divided."* Just like those two plumes of smoke, which had one common "origin," but were two separate existences. Harry and Voldemort share a mental core.

Is this how Dumbledore has been able to comprehend some of the really complex events?

—————— *Running Bits* (some tricky ones) ——————

BRAIN, MAD
"..."'completely **addled**...'"

RING, COLOR (SILVER), TWISTED/COILING
"...**silver-ringleted** witch..."

DUNG
"...*Entrail-expelling Curse.*"

————————— *Hints* —————————

✳ Items of Intrigue ✳

INFORMANTS Headmaster Dumbledore has his portraits to help him watch what is going on. Umbridge has her own crackerjack spies. HP Sleuths may have noticed the snitch (no big surprise) who informed her that the kids were up and in Dumbledore's office the night of Mr. Weasley's attack..

PORTRAIT LOYALTIES Whose side are the portraits on? Note: we were told whose side they are *supposed* to be on.

THE BITE Mr. Weasley's snake bite seems to have been a bit unusual. Maybe that is not surprising considering the snake belonged to Voldemort. Then again, HP Sleuths could be thinking Rule #4 as they diagnose this mystery.

MR. WEASLEY'S POWER How powerful a wizard is Mr. Weasley? He may not be feeling up to snuff, yet he gives a small demonstration as he plays host to a pack of get-well visitors. He likes to draw – which seems to be a favorite activity around here – just as it was for some treacle fans in *Alice in Wonderland* (who also had a preference for the letter "M").

GOLDEN FEATHER Fawkes delivers messages to the Order by leaving a single golden feather. Normally, you wouldn't focus on this feather, but as Uncle Vernon keeps pointing out, the magical world isn't "normal." What happens to this golden feather? Do they keep it? Does it have any special properties?

KREACHER For being such a helpless and demented house-elf, did you notice how Kreacher was having no problem being secretive and devious? His actions were stealthy and seemingly purposeful.

✴ Secrets and Concealed Clues ✴

ESSENCE DIVIDED The WWP Sleuthoscope is so stressed from trying to sit still that it's developing a splitting headache. This is one of the primary points to the mystery: "but in essence divided." If you can't make head nor tail of it, you can start, once again, by being a bookworm. Grab your HP Sleuth reading list and search for mysticism references or E.R. Eddison. You should also think about the related symbolism (two snakes from one) against your mythology references. (We have a message about a really big hint – think planets too!)

HOSPITAL LIGHTING The WWP Sleuthoscope is emitting little bubbles of frustration. The description of St Mungo's Hospital is both curious and conventional. The lighting was especially effervescent. HP Sleuths who read our previous Guide know what we think about the institution; now that you've had a look around, what do you think?

DISFIGUREMENTS We saw some really scary "disfigurements" in St Mungo's – especially if you are looking for clues. Your running bits could even help you here.

LEG PATIENT Check out the woman in Mr. Weasley's room with the "chunk" out of her leg, and keep it in mind for Chapter 31 {"OWLs"}. This is, of course, yet another major leg injury. It really smells but not necessarily like fish. Have you been keeping track of all the illegal creatures we've seen lately? HP Sleuths should have a trunkful of scrolls by now that relate to this.

MR. WEASLEY'S COMMENT Mr. Weasley was extremely concerned about those biting door knobs in the Daily Prophet article. HP Sleuths had better be too! You may want to reread very carefully to make sure you understand all the fine points since there are at least nine or ten clues you should find very handy.

THE HEALERS There are enough things in this hospital to make most HP Sleuths jumpy. The list of Healers is quite suspicious. We apparently have some background already on Hippocrates Smethwyck. Get out your *Philological Stone* and

Quidditch Through the Ages to find out more. (Hint – you are looking for *two* people by that name and the UK version has a different spelling from the U.S. version). The Augustus Pye person bothered us most. Not only is he an Augustus, but he is made of the same "stuff" as our Minister for Magic.

WARD NAME The ward in St Mungo's, where they visited Mr. Weasley, was the "Dangerous" Dai Llewellyn Ward. If you have done your required reading of *Quidditch Through the Ages*, you will know who "Dangerous" Dai was, and why there currently needs to be a ward named after him. There is yet more to the Llewellyn name that may be familiar to fantasy readers.

MUGGLE PATIENTS Muggles are frequently subjected to unfortunate encounters with magic (it's what ensures Mr. Weasley has a job). But this time, the Muggles who were attacked by biting door knobs were in St Mungo's. Mr. Weasley really wanted to see them. Are HP Sleuths checking their Rules?

———————————— ✳ ————————————

Chapter 23 Clues

(CHRISTMAS ON THE CLOSED WARD)

FAQs

WHAT DOES THE WORD "MATE" MEAN AND WHY DOES EVERYONE KEEP USING IT?

The twins are using the word "mate" constantly in Book 5, Ron and Harry seem to have picked up on it. Even the Mapmakers in "Snape's Worst Memory" toss the word around. What does it mean? There are several definitions, and if you've been paying attention throughout our Guide, you would know that J.K.R. means ALL of them. 😊

Twin, Twain, Two *(The mate to my sock)*
Friend, Fellow *(Me and me mates)*
Assistant *(I'm the boss...here's my mate)*
Significant Other *(Wife, husband, etc,)*
Procreate *(Make babies)*
Greeting *(Hey, Matey)*
Schoolmate *(Hogwarts kid)*
Checkmate *(Game of chess)*

So, why does everyone keep using the "mate" word? It's easy, mate, it's a clue that's double-trouble!

Running Bits (some tricky ones)

BUBBLES, BALLOONS
"....Memory bobbing to the surface..."
"...blowing gum wrapper."

SPOTS
"...pockmarked..."
"'They're freckles!'"

Hints

✳ Items of Intrigue ✳

SATSUMA VS WALNUT Some of the injuries that were described in the hospital seemed a bit absurd or for the dim-witted – such as the patient who had the "satsuma" stuffed up her left nostril. Oddly it was a "walnut" for U.S. readers. Whatever it was, it makes you wonder what those trolls would have been doing to get something that large shoved up their nose (ugh!).

GILDEROY'S "THERAPY" We hate to bring up the "C" word again, but the remedies for Gilderoy's condition sound *coincidentally* like the name of the remedy Snape dreamed up for Harry's "condition."

GUDGEON CLUE Here's a name that brings back fond memories of detention from years past. Since we hadn't heard from either of them for over a year, in our previous Guide we didn't reference the tie between Gladys Gudgeon and a certain student mentioned in Book 3, Chapter 10 {"The Marauder's Map"}. Since she seems to have taken such a long-term interest in Gilderoy, HP Sleuths need to keep an eye out for Gladys. ✒ *This is a whomp'n easy one...* ✒

MRS. LONGBOTTOM She may be a weird lady, but did you see the way Mrs. Longbottom addressed the kids? What do you think of her?

A ROUND TWELVE The running bit "round" was juxtaposed to the running bit "dozen" (12). What kind of image do you see this time when you hear the phrase "round dozen"?

✳ *Secrets and Concealed Clues* ✳

ALL HIS EGGS IN ONE BASKET The WWP Sleuthoscope is getting the idea that it could fool us (Not!). Harry comes to the realization that the "weapon" could be him. In fact, that is what the plot is all about. But then again, when has someone like Voldemort put all his eggs in one basket... and since when have HP Sleuths ignored Rule #4? CONSTANT VIGILANCE!

JANUS THICKEY If you are up on your *Fantastic Beasts* Trivia, you would know why Janus Thickey may have needed a ward. You may have also observed the (hem-hem) coincidence that there is more than one thing about this ward that's an imposter. (Hmmmm.... that word keeps coming up lately, doesn't it?)

DOBBY'S PICTURE The WWP Sleuthoscope is monkeying around a bit at the corner of the desk, hoping to catch our eye. Dobby probably isn't the best artist, but poor Harry doesn't even look human. What did Fred think about it? Maybe Dobby used a bit too much ink. No matter which way you stare at that ugly picture, there are clues popping out of it! HP Sleuths had better make sure they take a second look at that picture!!!

HOMEWORK PLANNER Hermione's annoying homework planner may not seem like it has any brains, but like *all* messages in Book 5, if you are watching for running bits, there's more here than meets the eye. Smart HP Sleuths may want to double-check your letters carefully and take its advice on penmanship!

AN EARFUL The old guy with the hearing trumpet makes us think about an author on the reading list who was deaf in one ear. Who else do we know with a bad ear?

KREACHER'S BEDROOM   It would seem that Kreacher's "bedroom" of a nest under the pipes is sinking too low for a house-elf of his background. With the whole house to himself, you would think he would want a better place. Yes, you would think....(hope that's what you're doing).

SPATTERGROIT   Ron may need the *Philological Stone* to understand what the healer said to him about "Spattergroit." Not only was his description of the symptoms a hidden clue – it is also a pun about Ron!

GILDEROY AND MEMORIES   Gilderoy's quill may have been in rough shape, but it still manages to draw vivid memories of slimy events.

Chapter 24 Clues

(OCCLUMENCY)

This chapter is double 12 – twice the septology intrigue!

FAQs

WHAT EXACTLY IS LEGILIMENCY ...AND HOW CAN OCCLUMENCY STOP IT?

We've been seeing what appears to be mind reading throughout the septology. In Book 1, Voldything clearly indicated that he can always tell when someone is lying; he somehow knew the Philosopher's (Sorcerer's) Stone had found its way into Harry's pocket from the Mirror of Erised in Chapter 17 {"The Man with Two Faces"}. Harry was already convinced by Book 2 that Snape could somehow read his mind about the flying car in Chapter 5 {"The Whomping Willow"}. Lupin was the scariest with the mind reading thing – he kept finishing sentences for Harry in Book 3 as he did in Chapter 10 {"The Marauder's Map"}. And in Book 4, Chapter 28 {"The Madness of Mr. Crouch"}, Dumbledore seemed to somehow know exactly what Harry was about to do (send an owl to Sirius).

Most of those could be explained as "great minds think alike," coincidences (hem-hem). Or, as we had rationalized, there appeared to be enough inside information that those weren't too difficult to deduce. However, we were sure that Voldything had some form of extra special powers. Now we know there is a magical explanation for all of them.

So, what exactly was the magic behind all this "mind reading"? We don't want any of you HP Sleuths to get detention from *Professor* Snape for not understanding the fine subtleties between mind-reading and what happened in those examples. Therefore, we will help by explaining the delicate distinctions between mind-reading and the skill of Legilimency.

"Legilimency" is the ability to access images, memories, and emotions from someone else's mind. Since brains are dynamic (thoughts are constantly being processed), and ideas and thoughts are stored in various forms (sights, sounds, smells, emotions, conversations, etc.), it is not possible to just enter a brain, search the index, and locate the information you are seeking. Also, there are typically higher emotions or more immediate/dominant thoughts that would get in the way of delving into specific thoughts you might like to access.

For instance, if you want to know something about Draco's next caper, but he just had the best birthday ever and can only think about his roomful of presents, then you may never get a glimpse of what you are seeking. However, if Harry is concentrating really hard on that Stone he just pulled from the Mirror of Erised, it probably wouldn't take any effort for Lord Thingy to observe that image in his brain. And the reason it works for lying is most likely because either the person is usually concentrating on the truth as they formulate the lie, or there is something else that happens when a person lies, which Voldything can detect (sort of like a magical lie detector).

It appears that there are some ways, however, to "trigger" a flow of memories. During Harry's Legilimency lessons, *Professor* Snape forced Harry's mind to replay highly emotional memories. Conversely, when Harry took control of their "mind link," it was Severus' highly emotional memories that were recalled. Even then, we are told, the intruder *doesn't* necessarily get to see *all* of those images either.

Voldemort has shown what a highly skilled Legilimens can accomplish. He was able to transmit the fake image of Sirius being held captive into Harry's brain so convincingly, Harry was unable to distinguish it from the real ones (see our hint below to get Lupin's opinion on who has the skills to combat the Master of Legilimency). That should plant some concerns in the minds of HP Sleuths.

"**Occlumency**" is the defense against Legilimens. If you want to block someone from tinkering with your brain, you need to learn Occlumency. The whole idea is to suppress your emotions and clear your mind. According to *Professor* Snape, controlling emotions is the key. That makes sense – as thoughts containing the highest emotions are the most accessible. The problem is, Harry was right – he wasn't receiving much help in learning how to block. However, *Professor* Snape was *also* right – Harry wasn't trying exceptionally hard either.

So, how does one become skilled in these subtle arts? Not by taking Remedial Potions. ☺

How does Voldemort Use Legilimency to Get What He Wants?

In Chapter 16 {"The Heir of Slytherin"} of Book 2, Tom Riddle/Voldemort tells Harry, *"I've always been able to charm the people I needed."* We now know from Book 5 that Lord Voldything's "charming charisma" was due to his ability to enforce his will on people through Legilimency.

Voldemort also uses his Legilimency to access information about people in order to control them. By knowing what people's deepest fears and secrets are, Voldemort can manipulate them. During Occlumency lessons, *Professor* Snape keeps telling Harry not to "wear his heart on his sleeve" – in other words, not to expose his emotional weaknesses. He explains that by doing so, Harry is "handing him weapons." Voldemort then knows how to get to him.

That may be how he controls his Death Eaters. It is definitely how he is getting to Harry. If Harry can't fight it and leaves himself open to Voldemort, we could end up calling him "Lord Potter."

What Did Harry See In Snape's Head (and Vice-Versa)?

What Harry saw:
- A young boy crying in a corner, watching a "hook-nosed man" yelling at a woman
- A teen with oily hair, shooting at flies with his wand, as he sits by himself in a dark bedroom.
- A "scrawny" boy, attempting to get onto a "bucking broomstick", watched by a laughing girl.

What Snape saw:
> Dudley and his friends harassing Harry during elementary school.
> Harry being forced by Dudley to stand in a toilet.
> Rookwood kneeling to Voldemort.
> Harry enviously eyeing Dudley riding his new bike.
> Harry being forced up a tree by Ripper, watched by the laughing Dursleys.
> Harry during the sorting, as the Hat recommends placing him in Slytherin.
> Furry Hermione, after the Polyjuice didn't work correctly.
> Harry being approached by Cho under mistletoe.
> Harry seeing a rearing black dragon.
> Harry watching his parents in the Mirror of Erised.
> Harry looking into Cedric's lifeless eyes.
> Watching the letterbox at #4 being nailed shut by Uncle Vernon.
> Dementors sweeping towards Harry (from across the lake).
> Harry being hurried by Mr Weasley down the windowless corridor.
> Harry approaching a featureless black door.
> Mr. Weasley diverting Harry away from the door to go left and downstairs.
> Gaping mouth of a Dementor.
> Snape standing in front of Harry.
> Traveling quickly through the corridor leading to the Dept of Mysteries, then going into the circular room illuminated by blue flames.
> Harry surrounded by doors.

———— *Running Bits* (some tricky ones) ————

2s
> "... big **second**-rater."

MOUSE/MICE
> "...the slight **squeaking**..."

FALLING BACK
> "...all **flung backwards**..."

VANISHING
> "...cheerfulness was **evaporating**..."

—————— *Hints* ——————

✳   **Items of Intrigue**   ✳

TITLE TRIVIA Pull your *Philological Stone* out of your pocket and use it to reveal the clue hiding in the title of this chapter. For this clue, pronounce the title word with the accent (emphasis) on the second syllable.

HARRY'S SECRET The "love affair" (choke) between Harry and Snape isn't getting sorted out even though they learn more about eachother. During Harry's Occlumency lesson, Snape may have gotten a peek at what seems to be Harry's most sordid secret – did you sense that?

SNAPE'S REACTION Did HP Sleuths happen to catch Professor Snape's reaction after seeing Harry's memory of Cedric's death? What would the master of Occlumency be thinking?

MADAM MARSH Where have we seen poor carsick Madam Marsh before? ⚓ *If you took the bus more often you wouldn't have to ask.*

PIGWIDGEON'S REACTION Pigwidgeon was very scared on the Knight Bus – just as Hedwig had been in Book 2 at the Whomping Willow. And Pigwidgeon had the very same reaction. Rule #3.

✳ *Secrets and Concealed Clues* ✳

DREAM ACTIVITY The WWP Sleuthoscope is turning green as it tries to stop from going ape! (Excuse us while we stuff it into our trunk... all the clues in this chapter, it could be too painful for it.) Snape explains that there are ancient charms and spells protecting Hogwarts from magical intrusion, and (as always) Harry's an exception. But if time and space matter, that starts to make us focus on some growing suspicions that we had alluded to about Harry's dreams as of Chapter 7 ("The Sorting Hat") in Book 1. They had been dormant in our minds until Snape just planted this humongous new clue and reawakened them. HP Sleuths should be aware that there is most likely a hidden link to all this dream activity that hasn't yet been uncovered. (Hint – use Rule #3 when searching).

CAST-IRON CLUES Look at those clues! The words "cast-iron," hidey-hole," and "vaulting" may not all be running bits directly, but look at their jux-ta-position!

CHESS GAME HP Sleuths who are big on imagery may feel right at home analyzing the chess game between Harry and Ron. You may want to have your thesaurus handy and think in metonyms.

LORD WHAT'S-HIS-NAME Snape's no chicken, so why is it he won't use Voldything's name and doesn't even want Harry to use it? Did you see the way he reacted as he discussed the subject with Harry? That hint should get your attention.

SEEING THROUGH SNAPE Lupin explains to Harry that some wizards have great expertise in Occlumency, and the better an Occlumens you are, the easier it is to fool people about your emotions. Now, what did Lupin call Snape? What questions (as if we needed more) does that raise about Snape's motives and loyalties?

FOUR LEGS AND A BANG With a loud bang, Sirius' chair fell back onto its four legs. Does it bring back images of Book 3 to you?

HEADLESS HATS Hermione is fascinated (Rule #4) by the twins' Headless Hats – she teaches us about the limits and capabilities of that magic. Hope you were paying attention. They reminded us of a certain helmet from Hades in classical mythology that was used in the wars with the Titans. You may want to search your mythology references for clues as to who used it for what purpose.

HEAD COUNT We think most of the danger is past, so we're pulling the WWP Sleuthoscope back out (it's promised to behave itself). Here is a NEWT–level question: How, how many heads have we encountered that have concerns about staying put? The clues in Book 5 tell us to keep *all* those heads in mind.

Chapter 25 Clues

(The Beetle at Bay)

FAQs

Why Did Augustus Rookwood have a different name in the UK Version?

On page 480 of the UK version of Book 5 (U.S. equivalent is 543), Augustus Rookwood was called "Algernon Rookwood." That is the only place in the whole book where that occurs. As U.S. readers know, it isn't that way in the Scholastic version, and it seems odd that with electronic search functions it would have gone totally unnoticed. We can't say that we know for sure, but we can say that looks suspiciously like a clue.

If it *is* a clue, the most likely reason it's there would be to point us to a certain famous author whose name has a familiar ring. A classic fantasy/horror author by the name of Algernon Blackwood wrote spellbinding tales about the interaction of the spirit world with our own. His stories include some titles that should twiddle the ears of HP Sleuths: "Dudley and Gilderoy", "The Willows", and "The Centaur."

Who are the known Death Eaters? (And Their Status as of the End of Book 5)

KNOWN DEATH EATERS	CRIME or EXCUSE	CURRENT STATUS
Avery	*Acquitted – Imperius Curse excuse (mysterious)*	Captured
Black, Regulus	*Wanted out, but was killed by a Death Eater*	Dead
Crabbe	*Acquitted – told Voldemort he would try harder*	Captured
Dolohov, Antonin	*Convicted – Gideon & Fabian Prewett murders*	Captured
Goyle	*Acquitted – told Voldemort he would try harder*	**At Large**
Jugson	*No info – was he a cry baby?*	Captured
Karkaroff, Igor	*Released – squealed on the others to get out*	**At Large**
Lestrange, Bellatrix	*Convicted – tortured the Longbottoms*	**At Large**
Lestrange, Rabastan	*Convicted – tortured the Longbottoms*	Captured
Lestrange, Rodolphus	*Convicted – tortured the Longbottoms*	Captured
Malfoy, Lucius	*Acquitted – bought his way out, Fudge implied*	Captured
Macnair, Walden	*Acquitted – Executioner for Ministry of Magic*	Captured
Mulciber	*Convicted – specialized in the Imperius Curse*	Captured
Nott	*Acquitted – told Voldemort he would try harder*	Captured
Pettigrew, Peter	*Never Fingered – assumed a victim*	**At Large**
Rookwood, Augustus	*Convicted – Ministry spy*	Captured
Rosier, Evan	*Died in battle – got part of Moody's nose*	Dead
Snape, Severus	*Not accused – Dumbledore testified for him*	??
Travers	*Convicted – helped murder the McKinnons*	Dead
Wilkes	*Caught in the act – Killed by Auror*	Dead

———— *Running Bits* (some tricky ones) ————

MOUSE/MICE, BABYTALK
"...wriggling and squeaking..."

BABIES
"...screechsnap seedlings..."

POKING, SPINDLY, EYES
"...looking bored..."
"...piercing stare..."

FREEZING
"...had become glacial..."

———————— *Hints* ————————

✳ *Items of Intrigue* ✳

DETENTION MARKS Harry isn't the only member of the "Resistance" to get the point from Professor Toad. You did spot that Umbridge seems to be giving out detention marks to other students, didn't you?

FABIAN CLUE Moody described in Chapter 9 {"The Woes of Mrs. Weasley"}, how Gideon and Fabian Prewett had fought so brilliantly. Hagrid had also mentioned their names back in Book 1 (Rule #1). If you look up the etymology for Fabian's name, it should give you an idea of how effective these brothers were at holding off Dark Wizards.

SNAPE'S LOYALTY Harry and Ron discuss Snape's loyalty with Hermione, who has her own opinions (doesn't everyone?). Right about now you should be thinking Rule #4.

DEATH EATER QUESTION Cho may not use her brain when choosing friends, but she does ask some intelligent questions about the Death Eaters. Have we yet heard any intelligent answers from anyone?

RITA'S INSULT What did Rita call Hermione? Is she ever going to learn? Well... a deal's a deal.....

✳ *Secrets and Concealed Clues* ✳

BODE'S KILLER The WWP Sleuthoscope is in such a state it is about to lose it's head (after we get done with it ☺). It is trying to get us to look at the septology clue about Bode's killer. What was done so far about the investigation into Bode's murder? Who are the suspects? (Hint – there are at least two possibilities in

Chapter 23 {"Christmas On the Closed Ward"}). HP Sleuths who have done their reading can track at least one of the suspects through the pages of *Fantastic Beasts*.

REACTIONS When the teachers at the Head Table see the news about the escaped Death Eaters, they are all stunned – except one. Those reactions (or non-reactions) should be food for thought.

HIDEOUT The WWP Sleuthoscope is starting to peer arrogantly at us. There are noises and screeches throughout Book 5, plus, we have a Shrieking Shack. Hmmmmm. Where would a Death Eater hide? If you had a Hitler-like army, would the Shrieking Shack have sounded like a good place? Maybe not for the whole army.... Maybe not even what you had in mind. HP Sleuths should scout for evidence that ties to these clues.

LOST LUNA Luna doesn't seem to even be aware what year it is as she dreamily stirs her cocktail. What clues do you think she is *holding*?

Chapter 26 Clues

(SEEN AND UNFORESEEN)

Double 13!! The WWP Sleuthoscope has a doubly difficult challenge! There are herds of running bits scampering sneakily through this chapter, taking the mickey out of all of us. This is one of the most important chapters in all of Book 5. It contains vital clues to the whole septology and is an aerial for all the other clues in there. Does the villain make an appearance here? Depends on how you define "appearance" – you could say it was a double vision.

CONSTANT VIGILANCE!

--------------------------------- *FAQs* ---------------------------------

WHAT IS SNAPE'S SECRET MISSION FOR THE ORDER?

At the end of Book 4, we were left with a Snape cliffhanger. Dumbledore said that *Professor* Snape was going to resume a secret mission of doing what he did last time to help fight Voldemort. Since we knew that last time *Professor* Snape had spied on Voldemort, it was a reasonable assumption that would be his mission this time as well. So we waited expectantly to find out all about Snape's secret mission. We're still waiting....

Although Book 5 has confirmed that Professor Snape is, indeed, working for the Order against Voldemort, it still doesn't answer all our questions. The first one that comes to mind (and Harry's too) is, what exactly is he doing?

We now know from *Professor* Snape's conversation with Harry in Chapter 26 {"Seen and Unforseen"}, that he is supposed to be finding out what Voldything is telling his Death Eaters *("That is my job")*. But we sorta already figured that out. The question is, how is he accomplishing it? There seem to be only two ways for him to do it. One is through Legilimency, and the other would be to physically appear when called (as a Death Eater).

It is possible that Snape *is* using some Legilimency on the Death Eaters to obtain his information. We have evidence that he is staying close to Lucius Malfoy (his subject?). There are certain comments that link him recently to Lucius Malfoy. One was Umbridge's remark in Chapter 32 {"Out of the Fire"} about Lucius Malfoy having "recommended" Snape highly. Another was Sirius' accusation in Chapter 24 {"Occlumency"} of Snape being Lucius' "lapdog," Remember – Snape also knew it was Malfoy who had recognized Padfoot at King's Cross.

There is also a chance that Snape could have been under a hood at the Death Eater circle in Chapter 33 {"The Death Eaters"} of Book 4. It would explain why Snape was so pale when he saw Harry's vision of Cedric's death (bet Cedric always got *his* potions right). Then again, if Snape had truly given up the Death Eater scene, why would he have shown up there?

Maybe he had no choice because of that mark on his arm.

Keep in mind, Sirius said his brother was murdered when he wanted out of the Death Eater business. As Sirius told Harry, *"...you don't just hand in your resignation to Voldemort."* So, how could Snape have done so? ...Or did he? We think not. We don't see how it is that Snape could have left and now be walking around free. If you recall from Chapter 25 {"The Pensieve"} of Book 4, Dumbledore testified to the Council that Snape had not quit, but had become a double-agent. He may have had no other option if he wanted to stay alive (that's assuming he's not already undead. Hehe).

Then, how does Snape masquerade as a Death Eater without anyone knowing? Snape, himself, has verified that Voldemort does know when someone is lying. *Professor* Snape is also a master Occlumens; he could be blocking his feelings so effectively that even Voldemort wouldn't be able to know his true loyalty.

So, is Snape still a Death Eater? Depends on whether you ask Dumbledore or Voldemort. The important question is whether he has really reformed, or if he is playing both sides? (hmmm...)

WHO ARE THE THREE DEATH EATERS VOLDEMORT HINTED ABOUT IN BOOK 4?

HP Sleuths have been debating this passage for three years. In Chapter 33 {"The Death Eaters"} of Book 4, Voldemort had slowly proceeded around his circle of Death Eaters, discussing his satisfaction with their performance. He personally addressed some of them by name, some he only referred to by their actions, and yet others he passed by without engaging in conversation at all. The most interesting discussion was when he stopped in front of an empty space where some of his Death Eaters should have been, and described the three who were still alive – one of whom was not there because he was (at that moment) at Hogwarts. (gasp!)

As we had just found out that both Headmaster Karkaroff and Snape were former Death Eaters, the status of these three missing members caught our attention. Voldemort did not mention any of their names, therefore we were left with another riddle to solve. This is all he said about them:

> *"'...One, too cowardly to return ... he will pay. One, who I believe has left me forever ... he will be killed, of course ... and one, who remains my most faithful servant, and who has already reentered my service.' 'He is at Hogwarts...'"*

The simple (and possibly the intended) interpretation is:

Cowardly = Snape
Left (be killed) = Karkaroff
Faithful Servant = Crouch Jr

The reason this would make the most sense is that Crouch Jr referred to himself as the "most faithful," and had been placed at Hogwarts by Voldemort. It was also common knowledge that the snitch (Karkaroff) had a bull's eye on him. That leaves Snape (or so it seems) – who could have been using any excuse to stay out of Lord Voldything's way.

Nonetheless, there are other logical scenarios, which should be considered. Although we don't know enough to be conclusive, we can profile each person in order to narrow the number of possible combinations. These are our assumptions for **Coward, Left service,** and **Faithful servant** – based on character information:

CROUCH JR

Coward – No, unlikely to be cowardly or mistaken for cowardly. Impersonating Auror Moody right under Dumbledore's nose was as far from cowardly as you can get (it even beats dancing in public at the Yule Ball).

Left – No, he was *in* Voldemort's service – even received a Kiss of thanks for it. Therefore, he couldn't be misinterpreted as the one who left.

Faithful – Yes and No, not necessarily faithful servant – may never have been a Death Eater. Daddy shipped him off to Azkaban without a trial, so we don't know if his conviction was only circumstantial evidence. Once in Azkaban, an impressionable kid, abandoned by his own father to be torment-ed by the Dementors, may have been easy mark for recruitment. He could have already been a Death Eater when they sent him away, but unless he was, he can't qualify as the faithful servant *"...who has already **reentered** my service."*

KARKAROFF

Coward – Yes, definitely the cowardly type. We saw him in action at the Yule Ball in Book 4: when in doubt...flee!

Left – Yes, you could say he left Voldemort's service. Disappearing without a trace does seem to qualify. Voldemort could not have been happy about it. Yup, dead Death Eater.

Faithful – No, not faithful. Nope, nope, nope.

SNAPE

Coward – No and Yes, could be coward – if that's the role he is playing to get out of being a Death Eater. Could also be crazed – double-agent between the two most powerful wizards in a century? Good act for a "coward."

Left – No, they probably still don't know he left (of course, we don't either). We were worried last year that he was a goner, but if that were the case, Malfoy knows where to find him, and Snape is still alive. (Then again, Malfoy did need a replacement servant boy.)

Faithful – Yes and No, another big...maybe, on the faithful routine. He seems to be hanging out with Malfoy, and he doesn't appear to be in any dan-ger. Guess that means the bad guys still think he's one of them? We have no proof (not even a teensy reason, for that matter) that Snape has given up all his evil ways. The only one who is convinced the master of Occlumency has defected from Voldything is Dumbledore. (hem-hem)

This is how it stacks up....

DESCRIPTION	CROUCH JR	KARKAROFF	SNAPE
Coward		X	?
Left / to be Killed		X	
Faithful Servant	?		?

As long as Crouch Jr was the faithful servant, there are no issues. He was most likely eliminated because either the Dementors were already receiving orders directly from Voldemort, or Malfoy was helping to cover up all knowledge of Voldemort's return – and we know how Fudge likes to make Lucius happy (jingle, jingle). Unfortunately, now that Crouch Jr can't talk, we also don't know if he had previously been a servant of Lord Voldemort or not.

If Crouch Jr wasn't already a Death Eater, then that could be really scary – as he doesn't even belong on this list! We would have to start looking for *another* "faithful servant' who had 'reentered' Volde's service at Hogwarts." It could be Snape, or it could be yet another unknown baddie (gulp!). Even if it's not Snape, Voldemort could still have thought it was, but why would he have talked about Snape as if he were already contributing to his cause? If Snape wasn't the "faithful servant," was he even the "coward"?

We had already suggested in our first Guide that it may not have been as easy as it looked. Book 5 throws a monkey wrench into the works. If there is any chance that Snape is still hanging out with the Death Eaters as part of his mission, then we need some answers before the mystery of the three missing Death Eaters is solved.

——— *Running Bits* (some tricky ones) ———

TONES, PIPES
> "...played the **bagpipes**..."

MARCH
> "...the **March** edition..."

HEMS, SKIRTS
> "...falling apart at the **seams**."

Hints

✳ *Items of Intrigue* ✳

GINNY'S SNITCH Ginny seems to have gotten awfully lucky with the Snitch, and is surprisingly confident about the Gryffindor team, wouldn't you say?

EXIT AT THE ENTRANCE Some people make a grand entrance, while others make a melodramatic exit. Trelawney's theatrics in the entrance hall should catch your eye as they are not as lame as they appear on the surface. You could call it a "spectacle" in more ways than one (hehe). It seems to be a clue in the form of an analogy for a famous entrance from a previous book.

SPLIT LETTERS The letters that Harry receives about his interview in the *Quibbler* are about equally split (sorta like many Book 5 clues) in their opinions. Some are "pro," some are "con," some can't decide, and some are from Paisley. (Hint – you've gotta think visually).

BLANK PARCHMENT The magic that students used to hide the pages of the Quibbler article should sound a lot like what was used to hide another sensitive document in Book 3. ⚑ *You'll get this 'cause you're probably up to no good... just like that greasy guy with the funny teeth.* ⚐

IMPERIUS CURSE Question: What can cause the Imperius Curse to be thrown off? Answer: Ask Bode.

OTHER EMPLOYEE We now know the whereabouts of two of the people who used to work in the Department of Mysteries. There should be a third around somewhere, if he hasn't croaked. Do HP Sleuths remember him from Chapter 7 {"Bagman and Crouch"} in Book 4? ⚑ *This is unspeakably easy – unless you've just crawled out of a swamp.* ⚐

SNAPE'S REACTION A quick quiz... Which makes *Professor* Snape more upset in *this* chapter:
    a) Harry peeking into the Department of Mysteries, or
    b) Harry peeking into Severus' childhood?
More insight into the Professor.

✳ *Secrets and Concealed Clues* ✳

DUMBLEDORE'S REASONS Why does Dumbledore want Trelawney to stay? It's far more important than just irking Umbridge – though that's definitely fun!

READING, RUNES, AND ARITHMANCY Hermione is reading up on potentially useful skills. What would they be used for? Well, you never know when you might run across a Druid or ancient Egyptian (this *is* a J.K.R. story, isn't it?).

AVERY Have HP Sleuths questioned how or why it is that Avery had such misinformation? You may want to do some background checking on this Death Eater. Chapters 27 {"Padfoot Returns"} and Chapter 33 {"The Death Eaters"} from Book 4 may will get you started.

SNAPE CALLS HIM THE "DARK LORD" Why does Snape call Voldything the Dark Lord? (Hint – look up Rule #2). However, you may get some ideas if you review our Hints on Chapter 24 {"Occlumency"} about his conversation with Harry.

SNAPE'S METHODS The WWP Sleuthoscope is sneaking stealthily across the desk but we're pretending we're not noticing. We have just enough information now to formulate some potente theories about the methods *Professor* Snape may be using to gather intelligence on Lord Voldything. Think in terms of what we discussed in the FAQs, plus his sharp mind, his odd mannerisms, his ties to certain people, and Sirius' discussion with Harry in Chapter 6 {"The Noble and Most Ancient House of Black"}.

TWO THINGS The WWP Sleuthoscope is now shivering so hard it is once again in danger of falling down and fracturing. It just can't keep still – maybe we should take the advice of the Rememberit Quill and stuff it down the toilet (although the stupid thing would probably just wriggle its way back up again). As you may have guessed, there are some monstrous clues here. For instance, we have a roomful of intriguing items, and when the Harry-Voldything looks into the mirror we see something very scary! Were HP Sleuths able to spot it? If you didn't get it on your first read, you may need to read a second. If the second doesn't help you, perhaps you can ask the Room of Requirement for research help – there are lots of tools in there to get you through problems like this. If all else fails, maybe you can find a friend to bounce ideas off. Sometimes two can work things out better.

WHAT SNAPE KNOWS How is it that Professor Snape says just a few words and a whole new mystery is born? Forget how Harry knows about *"that man and that room"*; start thinking about how *this* man (you know, the one with the dirty underwear) could know.

Chapter 27 Clues

(THE CENTAUR AND THE SNEAK)

FAQs

QUESTION: WHAT IS FIRENZE'S CLASSROOM?
Answer: A Holodeck
Question: What is a Holodeck?
Answer: Just like Firenze's Classroom

COULD DUMBLEDORE REALLY BREAK OUT OF AZKABAN THAT EASILY?

That's what he said, and we're not going to dispute it – so why are you looking here?

WHAT WAS IT THAT HARRY FELT BRUSH BY HIM?

Book 4 confirmed that you don't have to be in direct contact with the jet of a spell in order to feel its effects. In Chapter 9 {"The Dark Mark"}, when the group of Ministry wizards were all casting spells at once, Harry could feel a draft from the jets whizzing overhead. We also know from other incidents – like the spell Draco cast four chapters later (before he was turned into the "*amazing bouncing ferret*") – that a grazing spell can cut or burn.

In this chapter, when Harry felt something brush by him, it was a wisp of a memory spell that Kingsley muttered and slyly released. It was, in fact, this memory spell that Dumbledore referred to later, which prevented Marietta from remembering the information so she was unable to betray them.

Did you see Marietta's glazed eyes? That reinforces our lessons that by watching people's eyes, it is possible to know if they are being affected by memory charms, Imperius Curses, or other spells which influence the mind. According to what we've been told, while the memory is lost forever, the dazed effect of the memory charm passes. However, Imperius Curses, which are constantly in effect, will continue to cause the odd look in the eyes as long as the person continues to be under the spell. Note – it is also likely that the eyes will clear a little if the victim is able to fight the spell.

It appears that someone performed *another* spell in Dumbledore's office too. When Umbridge was shaking Marietta, she suddenly let go as if she had been zapped. This was the same kind of reaction Vernon had in the first chapter when he was throttling Harry at the window.

It was probably either Kingsley or Dumbledore who had stopped her, but it was Dumbledore who claimed the responsibility. Useful spell.

HOW DOES A PATRONUS GET ITS SHAPE?

Although the Patronus spell works the same way for everyone, the shape of the Patronus varies with each individual. The Patronus seems to be an extension of a person's personality. You can think of it as: "If you were an animal, what would you be"? The only difference is that you don't actually choose – it just sort of pops out.

There is a link here, again, to the portraits and to what Dumbledore saw in his silver instrument. For those who are into such things, you could call it an external manifestation of their psyche.

That means we can definitely infer things about people – based on their Patronus. Cho Chang's was a Swan – which implies that although she is beautiful now, she may have been an "ugly duckling" as a child. Philip Pullman developed a Patronus-like concept for his trilogy (see Suggested Reading).

———— *Running Bits* (some tricky ones) ————

NOSES, SPOTS/DOTS/INK
"...whose nose was now spotted with ink..."

9 OF 10
"...only ten to nine..."

HEART, POUNDING, MAD
"...heart drummed madly..."

———— *Hints* ————

✳ *Items of Intrigue* ✳

RUDE UMBRIDGE What did Umbridge call Marietta?

THE AUROR Who did Fudge bring to confront Dumbledore about the DA? Who did Umbridge bring to take on the demi-giant Hagrid? What did Dumbledore think about this Auror?

DUMBLEDORE'S POWER Does anyone have any questions regarding how powerful Dumbledore is? If so, are you sure you've read this chapter?

THE BELL That classroom bell was very jarring, wouldn't you say?

DUMBLEDORE'S PLANS Professor Toad wanted to know where Dumbledore had gone when he escaped. Maybe it's just as well she didn't hear what he told Harry.....

REQUIRED LIST When Umbridge needed to find evidence of the illegal meeting, she had Pansy Parkinson go into the room where she "conveniently" found the list of DA members. Some facts for HP Sleuths to consider.

PHINEAS' POPULARITY How popular was Phineas as a headmaster? (Hint – about the same as he is as a portrait.)

FORTESCUE Where have we seen that name Fortescue hanging around before? If you take a stroll through Diagon Alley in Book 3, you may run across him there.

✳ Secrets and Concealed Clues ✳

MIRROR, MIRROR WWP Sleuthoscope is eyeing itself in the mirror. Was Marietta that vain, or was it Harry's luck that she saw her blemished face in Umbridge's mirror? Why does Umbridge need a mirror? Is she able to look in it without cracking it? Maybe it's a funhouse mirror to make herself look taller. (snigger)

MARCH OF THE CLUES March is in the air, and HP Sleuths should be thinking very hard of March-type things. We are beginning to get the feeling that these clues are also on the march, and could become overwhelming very soon.

FORGOTTEN AGAIN It seems that Harry may have forgotten to use more than one mirror in Book 5. Shouldn't he have used one in this chapter too?

HEAVENLY EFFECT Firenze's classroom is a mind-boggling paradox. What did you think of that anthropomorphic effect in the heavens from Mother (or is it Father) Nature?

THE REAL STORY Fudge accused Dumbledore of inventing fantastic stories about Harry (punctuated by that stupid laughing of Percy's). Most of them should have been quite familiar, did you notice? It's just like Dumbledore to have told him the real stories, isn't it?

JOLLY GUY Fudge seemed to have been in a very jolly mood. HP Sleuths should flag this clue while going back and digging through Luna's Quibbler in Chapter 10 {"Luna Lovegood"} for other dirt on Fudge.

Chapter 28 Clues

FAQs

WHY DID SNAPE PUT HIS MEMORIES INTO THE PENSIEVE?

When we read about the Pensieve in Book 4, it was unclear whether the "thought" that was placed into the Pensieve was a copy or was actually removed from one's mind. We can now conclude that the memory is physically removed. Another issue, which has yet to be resolved, is how the "memory" is viewed in third-person (you can watch the person whose memory it is). That makes some difference when trying to understand what is "real" vs. what is only stored in memory.

Why does *Professor* Snape remove some of his memories before working with Harry? We know (from having seen it) that at least one of them was a very painful and degrading memory that he did not wish Harry to access. But were the others similar in nature?

We are thinking that there may have been several reasons that Severus removed those memories. In addition to the embarrassment of having Harry see the memories, it is possible that he didn't want Voldemort to have access to them either. They could be the kinds of memories and emotions that should not be accessible to a manipulator like Voldything.

The other memories Snape removed may not have all been personal. Instead, they could have related to the secret work that Severus is doing. It may have been random chance that Harry ended up seeing "Snape's Worst Memory" rather than "The Order's Secret Battle Plan." That could be the same reason why Dumbledore may not be willing to share the Order's plans with Harry! Since everything Harry sees is presumably accessible to Voldemort, the consequences could have been even worse than they were. But then, isn't Snape already of the opinion that rules don't apply to Harry?

WHY WAS JAMES PLAYING WITH THE SNITCH – DID HE PLAY SEEKER?

The jocks on a professional U.S. football team will play with a football – even if they are linemen who never touch the ball in a game (except when it pops into their arms!). Similarly, a goalie will run around with a soccer ball – even though all he cares about is batting it away during the game. It is a status symbol of their profession. Therefore, we cannot make assumptions about the position that James played solely on the basis of his playing with the Snitch.

Having said that, we do have enough evidence to question whether James ever played Seeker.

The only way we knew what position James played was from a chat with J.K. Rowling on Scholastic.com from October in 2000. She told us then that James played Chaser. However, in the first Harry Potter movie, there was a Quidditch plaque that had listed James as Seeker. And now we see him playing with the

Snitch.

Well, there is no reason to believe that he only played one position. In Book 5, Ginny is playing Seeker for the Gryffindor team and helped to win the Cup for them. However, she made it very clear to Harry that she would like to play Chaser *when* (not if) Harry returns to the team. It is very possible that James played **both** positions.

CAN PEEVES BE EXPELLED BY THE MINISTRY OF MAGIC?
How do you expel a ghost? We do have a precedent for the reverse of that. In Chapter 25 {"Egg and the Eye"} of Book 4, Moaning Myrtle described how she was "forced" by the Ministry to *stay* in her bathroom. We are not sure what would happen if she then tried to leave, but we know that they have some kind of "authority" to make her stay. So, if they can force a ghost to stay, why can't they force a poltergeist to leave? Even if they do have the right to make him leave, there is one sticky problem.... Where do you expel Peeves to where he won't create worse chaos?

--------- *Running Bits* (some tricky ones) ---------

JUMPING
   "...was jumping about..."

BUBBLES
   "...spitting out soapsuds..."

PAIRS/DOUBLE, 2s
   "...mate..."

----------------- *Hints* -----------------

✳ *Items of Intrigue* ✳

PUMPKIN HEAD We can see Fudge as a pumpkin head. If you've never made the acquaintance of a pumpkin head, you can introduce yourself to one in "The Land of Oz." (See your Suggested Reading).

STEBBINS Didn't we see Stebbins before at "The Yule Ball" with Fawcett in Book 4? We can't seem to remember the face....

JAMES VS. SEVERUS James explained to Lily what he thought Severus had done to him that was so bad. Do *you* know what he meant by "he exists"? Are you convinced that's a figure of speech?

✳ *Secrets and Concealed Clues* ✳

BIG LINK HP Sleuths should figure out what the house points here, in Chapter 38 {"The Second War Begins"}, and in OWL exams in Chapter 31 {"OWLs"}, have in common. ☺

READING RULE #4 Lupin and others (eg. Luna with her *Quibbler*) have pretended to be reading when they are, in reality, all ears on the nearby conversation. So, why should we assume that just because we are told that someone appears to be "reading" that they really are?

FIREWORK CLUES OOP! The WWP Sleuthoscope just did a little backflip to escape the rude fireworks (or was that about a bear on the corner?). If you want to watch the fireworks in *Order Of the Phoenix*, you had better bring your thesaurus, list of running bits, and *Philological Stone*! The running bits are as bad as the fireworks – there are so many packed in there, it's as if they're multiplying as we read them. While you're at it, consider if the Pensieve may alter or enhance memories in any way. Wish we could find one of those for ourselves...

LEGILIMENS THOUGHTS As Harry watched the fireworks from the dorm, he thought about Occlumency lessons and his stomach gave a "jolt." Guess his stomach doesn't like to think about them. Could his stomach be trying to tell him something *in particular?*

DUMBLEDORE'S WHEREABOUTS Umbridge sat Harry down in her pukey office to ask if he knew where Dumbledore was. Do you think he was nearby?

SEVERUS' MEMORY The WWP Sleuthoscope is fuming in indignation, but it will just have to let HP Sleuths work this one out for themselves. How many times did J.K.R. point out it was Severus' memory? What would that mean? How many times did she say that Snape was busy reading. What would that mean? How did everyone address each other? (hem-hem!) Also, what did James write on his paper and what would that have meant? (The meaning's easy – what you should be asking is how *Snape* knew?) HP Sleuths may want to review some of Book 3 while looking at this memory since it raises as many questions as it answers.

J.K.R.'s "JOKE" There's more smoke still coming out of the WWP Sleuthoscope... The scene on the lawn, from Severus's memory, needs to be read *very* carefully (as if you didn't know that). You should have your running bits reference chart and your *Philological Stone* handy when you do. Did you hear Peter's silly laughing at meaningless events? (We're getting irritated by stupid people.) Did you notice that advice Harry wanted to give James about Peter's antics? We think we'd better advise people about J.K.R.'s sense of humor!

✳

Chapter 29 Clues

(CAREERS ADVICE)

FAQs

WHO IS THE BLOODY BARON?

We don't know much about the Bloody Baron except that he's not the sociable type. Not only is he quite ghastly for the living, but even the ghosts are intimidated by His Bloodiness. He does attend the "ghost council" meetings, and we know he will even push his weightlessness around there. What we do know is that he is covered in blood, he is very mysterious, and he is the only one who can control Peeves the Poltergeist. That gives us a hint about the kind of living character he was.

There is one character that does seem to fit the description of the Bloody Baron quite well. In the *Contes du Temps*, by Charles Perrault, a character by the name of "Bluebeard" killed several wives all because they couldn't resist taking a peek into a locked room, which held the carnage of all of their predecessors. The way he found out they cracked was that once they used a magical key, they couldn't clean off (what else) the blood.

There is another strong candidate as a model for this gruesome ghost. The Baron Redesdale was an Englishman. Unfortunately, he was also a supporter of Hitler and anti-Semitic organizations. The Baron's whole family were in Hitler's inner circle... except one daughter. That daughter stood up for what was right just as J.K.R.'s characters are asked to do. That brave daughter impressed J.K.R. so much that there is now a certain link between her and J.K.R.

The Bloody Baron may not relate to either of these, but until we get more information, we feel they are bloody good possibilities.

Running Bits *(some tricky ones)*

BALLOONS, HEADS
"...bobbing overhead..."

MUFFLE, HOT, ROUND, HEADS
"...hot muffler around his head..."

DUCKING, CHAINS, BOLTS
"...ducked...*the heavy* chain *and* iron peg..."

Hints

✳ Items of Intrigue ✳

ANOTHER RON JOKE Did you laugh at Ron's far-fetched joke about winning the cup?

MORE JACKS Jack Sloper knocked himself out. Awww... Jack fell down. Did he break his crown? Time to get out your crib notes to find out.

UNSEEN When Harry went to put on his Invisibility Cloak in order break into Umbridge's office, no one saw him. Right?

SYMBOLISM If you examine the St Mungo's career literature, you may come across their logo buried in those piles of parchment. Check your running bits reference as you unearth a trove of images in that symbol.

TWINS' BIG EXIT It was a crazy scene when Gred and Forge made their big exit. Reminds you of an ancient ritual circle, doesn't it? Have you thought about where they got all the great props? (Translation – Stinksap-type goo.)

PIE FRILL Pie frills were the "in" thing in Nick's completely-headed time. Why are they in style for Umbridge now?

✳ *Secrets and Concealed Clues* ✳

ANYTHING'S POSSIBLE From having grown up with Fred and George, Ginny says she now thinks "anything's possible." What does she mean by "*anything*"?

THE ATTIC Kreacher may not be down to earth all the time, but have you questioned why he's hanging out in the attic?

Chapter 30 Clues

(GRAWP)

FAQs

WHY DID THE CENTAURS ATTACK FIRENZE?

As we described in our first Guide, the centaurs really do know what lies ahead. They differ from Trelawney and "fortune tellers" in that their divination powers are not only very real, but foretell events that effect all living creatures rather than individuals. Centaurs may not have been able to predict whether Binky the bunny was going to die, but they would know about the return of the most evil wizard in a century. They see major events – not necessarily on a day-to-day level, but over time – on a world-level. They have now clearly seen the signs of war as Mars brightens. (Did you know that, as we write this Guide, Mars is *truly* closer to us – and brighter – than it has been in 60,000 years?)

However....

The Centaurs are in some way sworn to not reveal the secrets of this power. Bane made reference to that in Chapter 15 {"The Forbidden Forest"} of Book 1, and now in Book 5, it was the cause of Firenze's banishment from the herd and he was almost executed for it! The reason could be strictly due to prejudice, due to an ancient pact that they are upholding through honor, or maybe by divulging the secrets, it would break an enchantment and they would lose the gift. By exposing the future, there is also a possibility destiny could somehow be corrupted by those trying to alter it.

We're in a bit of a fog as to why the centaurs are not supposed to share their knowledge, but what is clear is it is a brutally-guarded secret. The worst part for Firenze is that he is sharing the knowledge with a human (considered by centaurs to be animals in their own right), and therefore, unworthy of the information. The relationship between centaurs and humans is already tenuous, so any incident, such as this one, is enough of an excuse for them to justify bloodshed. Unfortunately, they are willing to kill Firenze for siding with a human (Dumbledore) – in spite of their knowledge that Voldemort is gaining power. Some more background reading on this can be found in your copy of *Fantastic Beasts*.

WHAT IS THE MEANING OF GRAWP'S NAME?

Hagrid relates how Grawp was (gulp) small for a giant. He had been teased and unloved by everyone – including his own mum. He has a very hard time with words, although as Hermy found out, he does try as best he can.

The Harry Potter books address intolerance on all levels, and show how much bickering goes on – even *within* groups who are suffering at the hands of others. The giants are exiled, without a true home. However, rather than unite and fight together, or unite and work out a contingency plan together, the giants just keep fighting among themselves – killing each other off.

Grawp is a child of this animosity. His name is highly appropriate in a story about intolerance, and is very sad. When Hagrid asked Gawp his name, it was difficult to understand what the little tyke said – but we were able to. Fans of Classic Trek may have already guessed it, or you can use your *Philological Stone* if you need help. If you think about the way he was always teased about how small he is, the only words the others ever used to him were:

"Grow up!"

─────── *Running Bits* (some tricky ones) ───────

BABIES
   "...foals..."

SPOTS, EYES, WATER
   "...spotted handkerchief - wiping eyes..."

PADLOCKS, CRACKING, EYES, MOUTHS
   *...her self-restraint was **bound** to **crack**...they had left the castle for **break**...she fixed Harry with a beady **eye** and **opened her mouth***

───────────── *Hints* ─────────────

✷ *Items of Intrigue* ✷

STUBBY TOAD Poor Professor Toad has so much on her stubby hands. Why would such an important Inquisitor have that much trouble removing a silly swamp? Harry was sure McGonagall or Flitwick could easily remove it. Doesn't her stubby little wand work? What could be her problem?

RON'S CUP If you reflect on Ron holding the Quidditch Cup, you may think you are having deja-vu. Where have we seen this image before? ⚓ *Unless you really desire to know, don't strain your brain looking for it.* 🪶

✷ *Secrets and Concealed Clues* ✷

PEEVES' IDENTITY The WWP Sleuthoscope just shuddered. What new information burst out at us about Peeves' abilities? This makes him even more complicated since he is both solid and ghost...yet neither. So, what is a poltergeist? With the help of Dumbledore's silver instrument, we at WWP believe we now know who and what Peeves is, and why he is allowed to flit around – making wisecracks and trouble for the living and the para-living.   Sci-fi fans can, once again, visit "Forbidden Planet" for hints (it's in your Supplies List).

MEMORY LANE Did you watch intently the *kind* of trouble Peeves caused? He was brilliant, wasn't he? Have we ever seen anywhere near that kind of trouble before? What do you think about McGonagall too?

HERMY Hermy's a cute name, isn't it? You might want to pull out your *Philly Stone* and see if there is a message in it. (Hint – your Suggested Reading could help clear up the myst on these mountains).

MEMORY TEST Hagrid had two black eyes. What else have we seen that might be described like that? ♠ *Don't bother trying this if your memory is failing.* ✐

AMBIGUOUS ANALOGIES The HP Hintoscope has suddenly woken up and started screeching like Sirius' mum, and now is blowing its crumpled horn. The WWP Sleuthoscope is scampering across the desk – it bounded over the inbox and fell over the edge (we think it landed in a cauldron we got from Dung). What drove it beserk was Harry, Ron, and Hermione were practicing on cups in Flitwick's class (btw – you should have recognized that pattern on the cups).

We can now practice our sleuthing skills too. There are several possible analogies for clues. The most obvious ones that work would use the cups to represent personalities, or the story line. However, there are both, hidden plot lines and captivating septology secrets in those crazy cups! HP Sleuths need to get out their magnifying glasses and look for anything – even Hair-Brain theories could be right. We can assure you, though, that the ones we're looking into are actually covering up the real tail in this monster book.

Chapter 31 Clues

(OWLs)

─────────── *FAQs* ───────────

HOW DO OWL GRADES WORK?

OWL grades are fairly similar to Muggle school grades. From what we have been able to determine, this is how the system works. There are five possible grades (If you don't count Troll):

Passing ──────────────────────────
        O = Outstanding
        E = Exceeds expectations
        A = Acceptable
Non-passing ──────────────────────
        P = Poor
        D = Dreadful

        (T = Troll ?)

For every passing grade you get, you receive one OWL. So, if you take ten exams and pass them all, you receive 10 OWLs. If you take 10 exams, and pass all but one, you would have 9 OWLs. If you take 10 exams and only pass three of them, then that would mean you would be Fred or George (3 OWLs each). ☺

The written exam for a class is worth one OWL; and the "practical" exam is worth one OWL; so, each subject is worth two OWLs. You can pass with an "Acceptable" or you can pass with honors ("Outstanding"). When the students went for careers advice, we saw that some of the careers required not just a minimum number of OWLs, but honors-status grades.

When they take their OWLs, they don't find out their scores immediately. Professor McGonagall advised them that they would not receive their grades until July (Book 6) – when they would be delivered by OWL Post.

HOW DID HARRY MANAGE TO MIX UP HIS PLANETS?

When Harry was taking his Astronomy OWL, he messed up the names of two of the planets before he noticed and corrected them. He had inadvertently marked Venus as Mars. If you are looking at the planets, that is difficult to do – one is brilliant white, while the other is bloody red. In fact, if you interpret it from the "classical" (or Luna's) perspective, it would mean he mislabeled "Love" as "War." Would that have been a Freudian slip?

——————— *Running Bits* (some tricky ones) ———————

WHEELS, ROUND
  *"...do some **cartwheels**..."*

UPSIDE-DOWN
  *"...**face-down** examination papers."*

CRACKING, HEADS
  *"...**landing loudly** on the thick **skull**..."*

——————————— *Hints* ———————————

✳ *Items of Intrigue* ✳

ORION Here is an Astronomy OWL quiz for HP Sleuths:
  1. What warrior is in the constellation of Orion?
  2. What is Orion's companion constellation?
  3. What is the brightest star in Orion's companion?

KIDS' STUFF In book 5, tableware are running bits, big dogs laugh, and moons mean wit. Where else would you find the answer, than in your reading list Kids' Korner? Animated tableware and fireworks should specifically bring up images from Looking Glass worlds.

EIHWAZ A missing "i" and the whole rune is ruined. (cough) Maybe Hermione should have taken the advice of Harry's homework planner? "Eihwaz" has ties to several clues in Book 5. HP Sleuths should have some luck finding clues by looking up the 13th letter of the rune alphabet.

BARUFFIO Where have we seen Baruffio before? The name reminds us a little of a buffalo we heard about in Chapter 10 {"Halloween"} of Book 1. ⚓ *If you have trouble with this one, I have some brain elixir that might help – only twelve galleons.* 🪶

TEA LEAVES Harry's reading of tea leaves for Professor Marchbanks seems to have been a bit flawed. ...Or was it?

BROOM CLOSET Why would Marchbanks look as if Dumbledore might come out of a broom closet? Why would Fred and George come out of a broom closet?

STRANGE WAYS Seamus has a strange way of studying. Then again, Harry has a strange way of listening to the news, doesn't he? (If you don't see the tie, you should review Chapter 1.) We hope by now HP Sleuths have checked out their copies of *Paradise Lost*, or you're bound to never see the light.

CURIOUS STUFF Ron turned his dinner plate into a mushroom. Here is an example of a J.K.R. running bits' headbanger. Consider the possibilities: fungus, toadstools, or the throne of a giant caterpillar (watch what you're eating). If you're confused, just take a trip through *Fantastic Beasts*, mythology, or *Wonderland* – where you will find some answers (but not necessarily be any less confused).

SECURITY BREACH What would have happened in 1749 to threaten the security of the wizarding world? Zoology buffs can grab your bloodhounds and follow Harry's instincts – you'd be on the right track.

NIFFLER ATTACK! We're not sure that *Fantastic Beasts* gives us enough information to shed light on this mystery of the ferocious Niffler. Was it true? We can't ignore Rule #4. Think...what do Nifflers do? Do we know what they eat? You should also check Rule #3 in regards to seemly-unrelated events in Chapter 9 {"The Woes of Mrs. Weasley"} and Chapter 22 {"St Mungo's Hospital for Magical Maladies and Injuries"}.

✳ *Secrets and Concealed Clues* ✳

RON'S VIEW You should focus on the somewhat confusing image of Ron's big save. He did have a little trouble resolving right from left, didn't he? You may need to view this with both your right brain and left brain to figure it out.

BUZZING SOUNDS Did any of you hear any buzzing sounds during the exams? HP Sleuths should know how much those bug us.

MIXED MEANIES Ron's worried about mixing Hagrid with monsters, but we're worried about what monsters have been mixing with metaphors. Scary stuff. 😊

MISSING PERSON The students were right in the middle of their exam when Hagrid was attacked, so they couldn't go anywhere. However, one person *seems* to have gone missing in the excitement.

OWL STRESS The students have lost their heads somewhat during the tests as their brains become a bit scrambled in the stress of taking their practical OWL exams. It seems almost unnatural how they kept mutating and multiplying their poor creatures, doesn't it?

Chapter 32 Clues

(OUT OF THE FIRE)

FAQs

IS IT REALISTIC THAT STUDENTS WOULD HELP UMBRIDGE?

The High Inquisitor deputized some of the students into her "Inquisitorial Squad" to oversee and report on the others. You can be sure she would have personally hand-picked the students who are sympathetic (or in Malfoy's case – enthusiastic) to her cause, are ambitious, or are looking for special favors. Those students are, therefore, even willing to overstep "legal" bounds to gain favor with her. This was a popular method of indoctrination for the Hitler Youth movement.

Percy's letter from Chapter 14 {"Percy and Padfoot"}, also employs a similar tactic, where he implies that Ron should rat on Harry. This undermines relationships and is difficult for anyone to counteract. Therefore, it is highly effective as a subversive strategy, and was used very successfully by Hitler to coerce children to turn in their own parents!

Hitler's "hit men" were Hitler's Elite Guard – like a "Secret Service" – otherwise known as the "SS." You never knew when they would pop up, and when they did, it was usually bad news (kinda like a Death Eater). Cognizant that there is a war about to start and Voldemort is recruiting troops, we can't help but think "SS" as we see all those double letters throughout Book 5. (Keep in mind – we're *not* implying that's the *only* explanation for the double letters.)

All of this parallels Hitler's psychological warfare techniques. Voldemort takes this one step farther through his brilliant scheme of using the media to discredit anyone who could be a threat. Thankfully, Dumbledore is also brilliant, and he's on our side!

Running Bits (some tricky ones)

INK, EYES
  "...smearing ink on the eyepieces..."

MUTTERING, BABYTALK
  "He was gibbering..."

WHEELS, ROUND, EYES (HURT)
  "...he wheeled around and strode blindly..."

TREES, CHAIRS, LEGS
  "...forest of chair legs..."

Hints

✴ Items of Intrigue ✴

LITTLE VOICES Harry's hearing little voices in his head that sound like Hermione (don't we recall Hermione's voice back in Book 2 saying it's not good to hear voices?) Our radar hasn't picked up any activity yet from the local brain, but we do advise HP Sleuths to keep an eye on her and to keep your own minds open.

KREACHER–LIKE CREATURE Where have we encountered someone like Kreacher who constantly talked to himself, served two masters (betraying at least one), addressed people in the third person, and disappeared – having lead his master into a deadly lair? (Check your HP Sleuth reading/movie list for *The Lord of the Rings*.)

SNAPE'S MIND Harry has always been an open book to Professor Snape. Why was he not getting through to Snape when he tried using Legilimency in Umbridge's office? Consider it to be a clue to Snape's mind.

✴ Secrets and Concealed Clues ✴

REPEATING MISTAKES The WWP Sleuthoscope is dimly flashing caution... Hermione was concerned that Harry was being led into a trap the same way he was led into the Chamber of Secrets. You are also being lured by J.K.R. throughout Book 5. Which traps have you spotted, and which ones will you fall into as you search through this Myst...?

NASTY RIDDLE Here's a riddle that may come in handy:

Who do we know that reminds us of Draco,
As he flips Harry's wand, just like some big macho?

DUMBLEDORE IN A PUB Umbridge thinks the idea of looking for Dumbledore in a pub is idiotic. Have you noticed that Umbridge isn't usually right about much?

✴

Chapter 33 Clues

(FIGHT AND FLIGHT)

FAQs

WHY COULDN'T HARRY SEE THE THESTRALS BEFORE?

According to Hagrid's lesson, you can only see Thestrals if you have witnessed someone die. Harry did see Cedric die in Book 4. So, if you have been wondering why Harry didn't see the Thestrals last year on the way back to the train, you are not confused; you are asking the right question.

In fact, J.K.R. was asked that very question when she appeared at Albert Hall only a few days after Book 5 was released. Happily she let us in on the "secret." You see, Hagrid forgot to mention something in his lesson – Thestrals don't instantly become visible. Why didn't Hagrid remember to tell us? There's a story behind it. J.K.R. had already written about the Thestrals in *Fantastic Beasts* because she wanted to have them visible to Harry. However, she decided that she didn't want to just stick them into the end of Book 4 without any explanation. There is now an extra detail about who can see Thestrals. At the Albert Hall appearance, she specified that *"you had to have seen the death and allowed it to sink in a little bit before slowly these creatures become solid in front of you..."*

Running Bits (some tricky ones)

FALLING, TRUNK, BABIES
"...a fallen sapling."

SPOTS/DOTS
"...peppering his enormous face..."

EARS, SCREAM
"...ear-splitting scream..."

STONE, WATER/RAIN
"...pebble-sized droplets..."

Hints

✳ Items of Intrigue ✳

TALKING TO THESTRALS All you have to do is tell Thestrals where you wanna go, and they'll take you there. (Cool!) More creature communications. More questions about creature communications.

✳ Secrets and Concealed Clues ✳

WHITE CENTAUR We were teased by the appearance of a snow white centaur. We were not given any name. Rule #2 may help explain this one.

CLUE REVIEW This chapter is a clue review lesson. There is not much new information, but all the most important running bits, clues, and hints are repeated in this chapter. We've seen them before, so consider this one big Rule #1. Grab your running bits reference card, and your *Philological Stone*, set your WWP Sleuthoscope on hyper-sensitivity, and have fun!

Chapter 34 Clues

(THE DEPARTMENT OF MYSTERIES)

―――――――――― *FAQs* ――――――――――

WHAT IS THE DEPARTMENT OF MYSTERIES AND WHY IS THE VEIL THERE?

By the end of Book 4, the only thing we knew about the Department of Mysteries was that the people who worked there were called "Unspeakables." In Chapter 6 {"The Portkey"}, Ron explained they are called that because no one knows what they do. It is definitely top-secret type of work that is perceived as scary or "out there." Everyone else is afraid to talk about *them*. Notice that in Chapter 7 {"The Ministry of Magic"} of Book 5, even the lift/elevator "voice" wouldn't say any more. (Sort of like talking out loud about You-Know-Who).

All throughout the Department, there is evidence of either scientific-type study or museum-like archiving. There are bell jars, tanks of weird specimens (even strange by Snape's definition), huge collections of timepieces of every nature, classroom-style rooms with multiple desks, archival shelving with carefully-preserved artifacts in a climate-controlled environment, and an amphitheatre-style room, which could have been used as a lecture hall or observation gallery. This Veil is apparently quite ancient – implying that it could have been one the "original" Veils, and is now housed and studied in the Department of Mysteries.

Even if it was not originally intended, the amphitheatre could, also, have been put to use for more sinister purposes. It has a bit of a Colosseum-like feel to it – especially since there isn't much to watch once a person goes through the Veil. Because some of the rooms on that level included courtrooms that hadn't been used in years, it is implied that it might have been tied in to trials and executions. Maybe it was used for capital punishment. We know the three Unforgivable Curses, at most, carry only a lifetime sentence in Azkaban. However, it is possible that wasn't *always* the case. At this time, we don't have enough evidence to say.

In addition to the observed evidence, in Chapter 37 {"The Lost Prophecy"}, Dumbledore told Harry that the room behind the locked door was one of *"the many subjects for study that reside there."* Nearly-Headless Nick also told Harry in Chapter 38 {"The Second War Begins"}, *"I believe learned wizards study the matter in the Department of Mysteries — ."*

There is no doubt that the Department of Mysteries studies really far-out subjects and is probably equivalent to Quantum Physics research by Muggles. Since we have already seen that they can control time, their study of it is probably quite advanced. If someone were to find a really odd object (such as a Philosopher's/ Sorcerer's Stone), it would probably be brought here for the experts to study. They are possibly even looking into the question of why magic exists (or maybe why some people are magical).

WHAT IS THE VEIL AND WHY WOULD HARRY AND LUNA HEAR VOICES IN THERE?

The "Veil" in the Department of Mysteries most likely represents (or is) the Veil of the Dead – a kind of "wall" between the living and the dead. The concept of a veil separating the two existences comes from the myth of the Egyptian goddess, Isis. A statue was placed in front of her tomb, in Memphis, Egypt, with the inscription: *"I am all that has been, that is, that shall be, and none among mortals has yet dared to raise my veil."* That was a very strong image in itself, but what has reinforced it are accounts about an incident with another Veil in the Bible, at the time of Jesus' death; *"And, behold, the veil of the temple was rent in twain from the top to the bottom."* Matthew 27:51. The Bible's Veil was similar to Harry's Veil in that it separated human existence from the domain of God while providing a portal for communication. From those ancient Veils has evolved the image of a "gateway" into the land of the dead.

It is possible that wizards may be familiar with the land of the dead and what separates it from the living. This particular "curtain" could be like a two-dimensional "hole" between the two universes (living and non-living). Philip Pullman investigated such a scenario in his *Dark Materials* trilogy. Before Dante's Inferno, tales of the "afterlife" focused on a wispy, shadowy "Underworld," where the spirits of the dead wafted through – somewhat emotionless, yet a bit morose. That was the "Hades" of Greek legends. If the souls of the dead are in there, then those would have been the "voices" Harry and Luna heard.

Classical mythology is full of people like Hercules and Ulysses who had visited the land of the "underworld" and returned. So, we know it has been and can be done. However, they walked in and walked out. Sirius was *"sent"* off to a place that we don't know anything about, so it may not even be possible to communicate from there, let alone return from there. Even one of his best friends, Lupin, was completely convinced he was gone for good. We don't know if he went to Hades or to some world J.K.R. has for dead wizards.

If the "Unspeakables" have studied the veil, how much have they been able to find out?

WHAT IS GOING ON IN THE BELL JAR?

The room where all the shimmering and ticking is going on is a room of time devices. The ticking is from the clocks, and the shimmering is coming from a huge bell jar. We are already convinced that the Department of Mysteries is where they study all the great mysteries of the universe. The presence of a bell jar with strange properties reinforces that.

Bell jars are most typically used by scientists to create artificial environments. This bell jar contains a closed loop of time – meaning events inside repeat themselves over and over – in a speeded-up state. As Harry watches the bell jar, he sees an egg that breaks open and releases a humming bird. As the bird drifts upward, it ages almost instantaneously...reaches an apex...and then drifts back down to the bottom of the bell jar. As the bird descends, it de-ages almost instantaneously, so that by the time it gets to the bottom, it has returned to infancy and is enclosed once again in the egg.

In our previous Guide, when we were talking about time, we had discussed in our analysis of Book 3 the paradox of "which came first...the chicken or the egg?" It seems that the wizards in the Department of Mysteries have been studying that. Is it possible that they have found the answer and J.K.R. is holding out on us?

WHAT DID THE INITIALS UNDER HARRY'S ORB MEAN?

When Harry saw his prophecy orb, there was a notation just below it. It had the cryptic message:

"S.P.T. to A.P.W.B.D."

If you had trouble figuring those out, you just had to think about who foretold the prophecy and who heard it. Those are just initials for the names of the people who witnessed the event. Why are there so many letters? We know from Harry's hearing that Dumbledore had a lot of names (as if Dumbledore wasn't long enough or hard enough!). The letters stand for "Sybil P. Trelawney to Albus Percival Wulfric Brian Dumbledore."

――――――――― *Running Bits* (some tricky ones) ―――――――――

STONE, FEET (MANY), MEASURE
     "...stone pit some twenty feet deep."

HOT/COLD, BLUE, WHEELS (HINT – THE ROOM IS ROUND AND YOU HAVE TO USE JUXTA-POSITION TO GET IT.)
     "...shivering blue flames on the walls and their ghostly reflections on the floor."

―――――――――――――― *Hints* ――――――――――――――

✴ *Items of Intrigue* ✴

LUNA AND THESTRALS Did you perchance see the Lady Luna riding the Thestral? What thinks thee?

HARRY'S TEMPTATION There have been several times throughout Book 5, including this pivotal scene, when Harry has been conscious of his Adam's apple (the little guy is growing up!). HP Sleuths should be conscious of parallels to certain internal struggles. Speaking of allegories... the orb room had a ceiling as "high as a church." Think temptation. Think "the right deed for the wrong reason." Are we thinking of Harry? If you don't know the reference, think about your reading list and T.S. Eliot.

BRIGHT IDEAS Have you had any bright ideas about why some of the prophecy orbs were dark? You can't be positive, but you should currently be able to spark some theories.

BLUE FLAMES We have seen blue flames in jars and on candles in Chapter 11 {"Quidditch"} of Book 1 and Chapter 8 {"The Deathday Party"} of Book 2. What do you sense was the purpose of the blue flames here (other than being yet another septology clue)? If you're at the door to the Department of Mysteries, you're getting warm. If you have made it to the high-ceilinged room, you're getting warmer. If you are starting to sweat as you're about to touch one of those warm orbs, you're toasty.

VEIL VOICES Harry and Luna seem to be the only ones who heard voices behind the Veil. If you're thinking Thestrals, you're thinking like we are. If you're also wondering about Neville AND Ginny standing transfixed, you are wondering the right things. As always, Hermione also seems to know when something's up.

SLIPPERY BRAINS Doors slide and brains think. So J.K.R. metaphors that speak of brains sliding should have you scratching your heads.

✳ *Secrets and Concealed Clues* ✳

STONE Stones were everywhere in Book 5. As a metonym, "stone" has an allegorical meaning which could point to the presence of a missing person. It can also evoke images of towers. Of course, Hermione may see it (the way she usually does) from a textual viewpoint.

VEIL DESCRIPTION The veil was described as fluttering "as though it had just been touched." Great analogy. But in Book 5, you can't even trust an analogy to be what it seems.

X MARKS THE SPOT Clever Hermione makes sure to mark the spot. The first time it is mentioned, it is a "fiery X", however, later mentions use the word "cross." Because J.K.R. was careful to draw it for us, we are sure the "X" is the primary interpretation, however, we see big clues looking at it from all orientations (including Luna's). For the alternate perspective, HP Sleuths can find reference material in their reading list under Leonardo da Vinci and Michaelangelo (see Suggested Reading).

Chapter 35 Clues

(Beyond the Veil)

FAQs

What Color Was the Spell that Hit Sirius?

If you read very carefully, you will confirm that we have no idea what color the spell was that knocked Sirius through the Veil.

> *"Harry saw Sirius duck Bellatrix's jet of red light: he was laughing at her...The second jet of light hit him squarely on the chest."*

There are *two* ways to interpret this. Either it was *another* jet of the same color which would have been red; or it was just another jet of light (unknown color). It was not specific, so it could just as easily have been a jet of purple or even green. From the way Harry reacted, however, we are led to infer that it probably wasn't green after all. If Harry was expecting a still-lively Sirius to emerge from the other side, it doesn't seem likely that it was green, or Harry would have been far more sure of Sirius' death.

If that spell wasn't a killing curse, does that make him any less dead? Probably not. Could it make him less "properly" dead? Possibly.

According to a WBUR radio interview with J.K.R. in 1999, people can't come back to life if they are *"**properly** dead."* Notice how she specifically left the door open with that modifier. So, knowing J.K.R.'s knack for twists, until we have confirmation either way, we're with Harry – we're not convinced.

Running Bits *(some tricky ones)*

Doors, Ceiling (it's a homophone)
"...**sealing** the doors..."

Measure
"...move **an inch**."

Babytalk
"...mock **baby voice**."

Hints

✳ Items of Intrigue ✳

Reinforced running bits There are a couple of nasty near-misses in Book 5. Sirius and Neville both almost made it into the running bits.

Seams odd It seems that Neville tore a seam. Although it may be nothing, the details of that do seem odd.

PLUTO Luna blew up Pluto. Sounds like something out of mythology doesn't it? Was that significant? What were they doing near Pluto?

BAD BLOOD Sirius' death at the hands of Bellatrix shows the extent of the animosity created by the pureblood bigotry. We know these two weren't kissing cousins, but do you think Phineas will approve?

✳ *Secrets and Concealed Clues* ✳

EVASIVE MANEUVERS Note the small detail about what happened to Harry in the confusion as the kids smashed the shelves and scattered. (Peeves would have been proud).

SOLSTICE PROPHECY Harry heard one of the smashed orbs give a prophecy about the solstice. Should we be thinking about June of 2003 (also known as Rule #3)? Will there be something happening in June of 2004 (WWP breaks out into a sweat and starts to keel over) or 2005? Or maybe we should be thinking about the *other* solstice? (makes us shiver)

TRAGIC EVENTS The WWP Sleuthoscope is waddling around the desk as if it's about to fly off in excitement. Sirius falls back through the Veil "in a "graceful arc" – like a reverse swan dive that seemed to Harry to take an "age" to happen. That sort of reminds us of the hypothesized effects of a physical phenomenon called an "event horizon." It also has an uncanny resemblance to a passage we discussed in the Book 4 Analysis of our previous Guide. HP Sleuths should review our comments about the twins where we review Book 4, Chapter 7 ("Bagman and Crouch"). You may want to spend some time observing this.

JUX-TA-POSITION! When you see the phrase: "*...they were mere feet away from Harry and the others...*" – use your running bits references (remember – the card doesn't have everything, so use the list too) and apply Juxtaposition!

TURNTABLE The way the circular room works should remind HP Sleuths of another room in the Department of Mysteries. Think about the number of doors, and think about how the room is turning. If you get an image that way, then it may lead you to other clues as well. You can also think in longer terms and more ancient terms. You can also literally think in two dimensions.

NEVILLE'S WAND Neville's wand broke. That's really terrible. ...Or is it? It was an important family heirloom, but was it really *Neville's* wand? What do you think Mr. Ollivander would say? We can't wait to see Neville with a new wand.

THE DOOR IS... When is a door not a door? When it's a joke... or when it's a running bit (otherwise known as a big clue).

MIA Where did everybody go? Hope HP Sleuths knew to keep your eye on Ron, Ginny, and Luna at all times.

DÉJÀ VU ALL OVER AGAIN Book 5 just keeps bringing us back to other sights and sounds in the first four books. Compare these two passages:

> "... don't be dead – please don't be dead – "

> "Don't let her be dead, don't let her be dead. . ."

FAMILIAR SOUNDS Let's see...a female with a bad foot...and a veil of the underworld. Now that has a familiar note. You may want to sneak a look back at your Greek mythology references for a tragic connection.

Chapter 36 Clues

(THE ONLY ONE HE EVER FEARED)

$\ast$

FAQs

WHAT COULD BE WORSE THAN DEATH?

Ron comments that there can't be anything worse than death. In Chapter 36 ("The Only One He Ever Feared"), Dumbledore tells Voldemort that *"there are other ways of destroying a man."* This feels like a Rule #1 to us. We are being told to start thinking about ways of destroying Voldemort other than just killing him (that didn't work the first time anyway). In our first Guide, we wondered what those echoes from his own wand would do to him, if they could. (smirk)

According to Dumbledore, there are definitely fates worse than death. In fact, literature is full of the possibilities. Many authors have envisioned horrible destinies that involve continuous torture. However, our favorite is not something Bellatrix would do, but more like something Gred and Forge might dream up. If HP Sleuths want to see a humorous literary perspective on the enticing possibilities that await Voldything, you should peruse a French classic called *No Exit* (*Huis Clos* in French). It's on your HP Sleuth reading list.

WHAT HAPPENED TO VOLDEMORT AT THE END OF THE DUEL?

Voldemort was at the fountain as this first battle between the two great wizards was ending. Dumbledore managed to cocoon him in the water – completely encased Voldemort (think chocolate dip) which became a shield as it was smothering him on all sides. It prevented Voldemort from being able to get at Dumbledore or anyone else with his wand, but it didn't prevent him from doing magic. If you look at the description of the Lethifold attack in *Fantastic Beasts*, you will get an idea of what Voldemort went through as Dumbledore's water attacked him.

Voldemort was able to do magic on himself in order to Disapparate or dematerialize (we weren't told exactly how), and left the scene temporarily...only to reappear *inside* Harry. Dumbledore was most afraid at this point when he couldn't see Voldemort. Possibly because he couldn't look at Voldemort and anticipate his next move, or because he had a feeling that Voldemort might try doing exactly what he did – take over Harry's body.

WHY DID VOLDEMORT POSSESS HARRY AND WHAT MADE HIM GO AWAY?

Voldemort doesn't gain pleasure out of torturing people (unlike the toad lady). The reason Voldemort inflicts pain on others is because he wants to control them, and that is his method of doing so. Although Voldemort can clearly do whatever he wants to other wizards, he prefers to manipulate them in order to achieve his ends. (When your "ends" are immortality and ultimate rule of the magical world, it's definitely a waste of brain cells to bother zapping peons unnecessarily.)

Anyone that gets in the way of Voldemort's achieving his ends (e.g. Lily) is controlled or killed. Since he can't control Dumbledore, he would like to kill him. Voldemort makes use of any opportunity to get what he wants, and what he wants is Harry – his primary obstacle.

Voldemort is exceedingly brilliant. In this battle, when he realized that he couldn't bypass Dumbledore to get to Harry, he *became* Harry. By possessing Harry and attacking, then Dumbledore is forced to defend himself. Voldemort gave Dumbledore a horrible dilemma – whether to shoot spells at the VoldeHarry (Harry's body) or let Voldemort attack him. Either Harry or Dumbledore would have suffered. Wonder what he would have done? (He probably had something clever in mind but he never had to go there.)

Harry was in excruciating pain from the possession. On the other hand, Harry's intense emotions about Sirius were excruciatingly painful to Voldemort. Voldemort could not inhabit Harry's body when he was that filled with love and emotion... so Volde flew the coop.

WHY DIDN'T HARRY'S CRUCIO CURSE WORK?

If you will search through your trunk of sleuthing scrolls and pull out the ones from Book 4, you can probably find the answer. Imposter Moody had told Harry's class that it took more than just uttering the spell. The lesson we are given is that Magic is not just words but the power behind the words. That would explain why some wizards are stronger than others. Imposter Moody had said that even a whole classroom full of students uttering the spell at him wouldn't *"get so much as a nosebleed."* So are we surprised that Harry couldn't pull off an evil curse?

HOW DID THE STATUES IN THE FOUNTAIN "COME ALIVE"?

This was not simple to spot, because it was done so stealthily that even Voldemort didn't notice! The statue that jumped in front of Harry caught Voldything completely off-guard. Dumbledore had sneaked up on him and cast the spell in time to save Harry. Then Dumbledore casually Transfigured the rest – just like McGonagall had done with the Wizard Chess set in Book 1. How interesting that Voldemort couldn't stop Dumbledore's fountain army. Yet, what we found most intriguing was how the statues were able to walk off to another part of the building in order to get Fudge.

——————*Running Bits* (some tricky ones) ——————

MUFFLED, BELL, RING
    "Be quiet, Bella..."

FALLING BACK
    "...lay flat on his back"

Hints

✳ *Items of Intrigue* ✳

THE OTHER DEATH Did HP Sleuths see the life-cycle themes and comprehend the loyalty shown in the second death during this battle at the Ministry?

THE ROOM RESPONDED Think about the ramifications of the revolving room responding to Harry's request... or maybe we don't want to know?

APPARATING SOUNDS What noise does Voldemort make when he Apparates? (Hint – what sound does Dumbledore make?)

HARRY'S SAVIOUR Were you conscious of the position that the statue took to save Harry's life as it took the spell full in its chest? No imagery there. ☺

✳ *Secrets and Concealed Clues* ✳

GONNGGG Dumbledore's spell made a "Deep gong" when it hit Voldemort's shield, but no damage was done to it or the space around him. If you're a scientist, you have to ask where all that powerful magical energy went. When trying to fathom what happened, it may help to look into "The Willows" by Algernon Blackwood or to contemplate space from a *Doctor Who* perspective.

Chapter 37 Clues

(THE LOST PROPHECY)

FAQs

HOW DO WE KNOW THAT WAS THE EXACT WORDING OF THE PROPHECY?

If you are asking this question, you are thinking correctly. The Pensieve is a container – it holds thoughts from people's minds. It would seem that those thoughts could only be as accurate as the person's memory of them. So, how can we be sure that Dumbledore remembered the precise wording? We have no proof, but we do have Dumbledore's statement from Chapter 37 {"The Lost Prophecy"}: *"...the prophecy was made to somebody, and that person has the means of recalling it perfectly."*

How does Dumbledore recall it "perfectly"? Is that the same talent Hermione used when she recalled the exact wording of Umbridge's speech? Or Is it possible that the power of the Pensieve includes the ability to guarantee a perfect recreation of the event as it truly happened? We don't know – we just have to take the Headmaster's word for it (that doesn't mean we packed away our fishing rods).

WHAT IS THE "POWER" THAT HARRY POSSESSES WHICH VOLDEMORT DOES NOT?

The clues to this "power" seem to be the spell of **love** Lily cast on Harry as she died, the emotion Harry had for Sirius, and Dumbledore's words, *"It was your heart that saved you."* If we take the clues literally, we assume he means the power of *love*. It is this power of love that Dumbledore discussed with Harry at the hospital in the last chapter of Book 1.

However, we have some contradictory information that seems to imply it is either more than love, or even something beyond love. In Book 5, Dumbledore describes this power as, *"...a force that is at once more wonderful and more terrible than death, than human intelligence, than the forces of nature."*

If HP Sleuths recall from the hospital scene in Book 1, Dumbledore talked about **truth** in the same way that he talked about the power of love here, *"The truth...is a beautiful and terrible thing, and should therefore be treated with great caution."*

Does Dumbledore really mean that love is *"...more wonderful and more terrible than death"*? Does he mean truth? Truth and love have been known to be equated. It is also possible that he means something else completely or even a combination of emotions. We have assembled a list of possible interpretations for the "power" that Dumbledore described:

Chivalry	Faith / Faithfulness	Loyalty
Compassion	Goodness	Love
Courage	Guilt / Remorse	Nobility
Emotions	Life	Truth / Honesty
Honor		

DOES SOMEONE REALLY HAVE TO DIE IN ORDER TO FULFILL THE PROPHECY?

Dumbledore says the "only chance of conquering" Voldemort is in this prophecy. It seems that he believes it too – since he didn't even try to kill Voldemort in their duel. Can this indicate that Dumbledore feels it unwise to meddle with prophecies, or does he have something more sinister in mind?

The prophecy talks about "vanquishing" the "Dark Lord." We need to think about those words carefully. Does it have to be a death, or can someone just "*Evanesco!*"? We'd like to see a way around this murder paradox, but prophecies can be tricky things (Oedipus can attest to that).

The prophecy also states, "*...either must die at the hand of the other...*" – that's pretty definite in our opinion. However, you don't have to take our word for it. Dumbledore reinforces that in order to fulfill the prophecy, someone has to be killed. Harry asked him, "'*...does that mean that . . . that one of us has got to kill the other one . . . in the end?*'

'*Yes,*' said Dumbledore."

(Note the tear as well.)

Running Bits (some tricky ones)

KINGS, CHAIRS
"...throne-like chair..."

DUNG
"...trapped in the bowels..."

COLOR (SILVER), INK
"...silver ink pot..."

Hints

✳ *Items of Intrigue* ✳

EAVESDROPPER Dumbledore said there was an eavesdropper who heard part of Trelawney's prophecy. Knowing how all things interrelate in a J.K.R. story, you should be questioning how he was discovered, and what happened to him.

HEADMASTER PORTRAITS We are told that "many" of the portraits welcomed Dumbledore back. Right about now you should be thinking of a glass of water. (Hint – half full vs. half empty.)

PHINEAS' REACTION Phineas goes to verify that Sirius is truly dead... Why does he have to verify? *How* does he verify? (Don't forget the "little" detail back at the ranch...)

KREACHER'S KONDUCT What is Kreacher capable of? Is he not a creature with feelings? Maybe not this Kreacher – did you see that he was able to inflict pain on another creature? Bad sign.

IMPLICATIONS OF SIRIUS' DEATH Here's an issue that could keep HP Sleuths busy until J.K.R.'s next book comes out: What are the implications of Sirius' death on his relatives? On the Order? On Kreacher? On his estate? (Hint – this is a big clue – you might want to look below the surface a bit on this one.)

✳ *Secrets and Concealed Clues* ✳

THE WEAPON X2 Once more we will ask HP Sleuths: Was Harry THE weapon? If you have to ask why we keep asking, then you haven't reviewed your Rules lately.

THE TRUTH Dumbledore told Harry that Snape gave him fake Veritaserum. Is that verified?

SNAPE AND DUMBLEDORE So far, Dumbledore has been right about everything – including Harry's scar. However, we also know from Book 1 and Book 4 that he can be fooled by very clever wizards. We keep thinking about what Lupin called Snape in Chapter 24 {"Occlumency"}. If you think about how that could affect Dumbledore, it could give you nightmares.

HARRY'S GUILT Did you see that painful-sounding metaphor (hope that's what it was) about Harry's guilt as a "parasite" that was eating his heart out? It was so bad that Harry was wishing he was someone else. HP Sleuths might want to start looking into fairy godmothers.

COMMUNICATION METHODS We may already have some shards of evidence about the Order's "reliable methods" of communications.

WIZARD CHAIR The Wizard in the portrait was seated in a "throne-like chair." If you know how this fits into the running bits, you are a king among HP Sleuths – an HP Super Sleuth for sure!

SMASHED PROPHECY So, the Prophecy was smashed. Now Voldything won't ever know the whole prophecy, right? Think hard... This seems to be a twist on a twist.

DUMBLEDORE RELATES Have you noticed Dumbledore seems to relate amazingly well to what Harry's going through concerning Sirius' death?

DUMBLEDORE LOOKING AT HARRY There is something about the way Dumbledore is looking at Harry. We know he has some Legilimency ability, but is that what he is up to?

WHO WILL KILL & WHO WILL BE KILLED Have you really contemplated what the prophecy means about who has to kill whom? We would like to point out that thinking outside the box may come in handy for this one.

SUNLIGHT SHINING Did you notice a little light on the subject on Dumbledore's desk?

THREE TIMES DEFIED The prophecy said that the "marked" child had to be the offspring of those who had three times defied Voldething. Supposedly both Harry's and Neville's parents had defied him three times. Somehow, we feel a big story developing here – don't you? We'll meet you in line for Book 6...

————————————✳————————————

Chapter 38 Clues

FAQs

IF HARRY MUST KILL VOLDEMORT...
WOULD YOU CONSIDER HIM TO BE A MURDERER?

J.K.R. teaches us that the choices we make define who we are. What if the choices are to kill or be killed? What are Harry's choices now? He is the only one who can stop the worst Dark Wizard in a century, but in order to do that, he must be a murderer. He can save many lives and much pain just by killing one terrorist. If he kills, is he a murderer or savior? As a baby who didn't know any better, his protection temporarily defeated Voldemort and made him into a hero. If he now kills with the knowledge that he is doing so, will he still be a hero?

If you think he should only kill if attacked, then should he be at a disadvantage and become a sitting duck? Or should he go after Voldemort? Is Harry really responsible to the whole world for this terrorist? If everyone knows Harry is the only one who can kill Voldything, then what should be the focus of their resistance?

WHAT DID NICK MEAN ABOUT "DECIDING" WHETHER TO GO ON?

You may feel sad, but Muggles now know that death is final for them. Only wizards can come back as ghosts. That is definite. Nick seems to be caught in a limbo between "here" and "there," and he isn't privy to what "there" actually is. By choosing to stick around, he has ended up being caught in-between. Nick doesn't appear to be happy with his situation. Although the living want to see people come back as ghosts, the ghosts seem to be trapped for eternity on earth yet without a true existence. It almost seems as if we could be considered selfish for wanting to keep them here. They are no longer part of this existence, and they need to go on to the next plane. Their decision to stay is a bondage – not a benefit. If you want to see how the subject is dealt with cleverly and humorously – scare yourself up a copy of *The Time of Their Lives*, starring Abbott and Costello.

WHY DID VOLDEMORT CHOOSE HARRY?

Lord Voldything thinks he is the most powerful wizard in the world. He was informed that someone could be good enough to challenge him. When he evaluated Neville against Harry, he chose the one who seemed to be the biggest threat. The similarities between the two of them were striking, and that triggered the "red flag" in Voldemort's mind. He was prepared to see a carbon-copy of himself when Harry grew up. But as we know, that wasn't the case at all. Nonetheless, the similarities (translation: coincidences) are definitely there. It just so happens that there is another (ahem) coincidence. There is at least one more person who uncannily resembled Voldemort. His name was Hitler.

Running Bits (some tricky ones)

SPOTS
*"...a **marked** man."*

9 OF TEN
*"...platforms **nine** and **ten**..."*

EYES, GLASS (USE JUXTAPOSITION AND YOUR PHILOLOGICAL STONE)
*"...**looking up** at the hour **glasses** on the wall..."*

Hints

✳ *Items of Intrigue* ✳

HE'S BACK The statement made by the Daily Prophet was that Voldything "returned" to their country. Odd way to phrase that, isn't it?

DEMENTOR WHEREABOUTS There are several unsettling questions to be answered about the Dementors' revolt at Azkaban.

NEVILLE'S GREEN THUMB Neville's Mimbulus Mimbletonia is getting to be a big guy (wonder if it's been outgrowing its pot?). You should also question whether it is a flowering plant. We are sure you saw that the plant was "crooning" as it was stroked. Is it crooning in Assyrian or does Neville speak Mimbletonian?

SWAMP OF AGES Prof. Flitwick left a "monument" to Gred and Forge by not removing all of the swamp. Stone monuments do tend to hang a round – sometimes for centuries. We see it as the Umbridge Memorial Swamp.

MONSTROUS MYSTERY SOLVED If you check the description of people swimming in the lake, you will see that settles one monstrous mystery.

BREAKOUT PLANS Draco always prides himself on inside information and being very well-informed, so when he brags about his incarcerated dad, we should heed claims.

SOMEONE HELPED Grawpy's doing surprisingly better. If you think about what may have happened in the forest, maybe it shouldn't be that big a surprise?

EXPERIMENTAL MAGIC Looks like Voldything isn't the only one who likes to experiment with spells. We now know from Luna that there could be a lot of that going around...

NAIL-BITER Hermione states that things with Volde will start happening soon. Rule #4 says that we had better make sure our survival supplies are well stocked.

MISSING UN-PERSONS We haven't seen much of the ghosts lately (yes, it's suspicious). What *do* ghosts do in their spare time?

✳ *Secrets and Concealed Clues* ✳

CALLING SIRIUS Although it seems unlikely that the mirror would work, did Harry even call for Sirius correctly? The mirror is smashed. What does that mean? Better check your crib notes and your scrolls for the lessons you learned in Book 5...

WAKEUP CALL HP Sleuths should be prepared; Harry is feeling like a different person now. Last thoughts can hold a lot of meanings (especially when they're J.K.R.'s) – and not all of those meanings are necessarily good...

LUNA'S HUNTING TRIP Luna is going on a safari this summer. How utterly exciting. (We really need to join her, you know – there's probably a lion that needs tracking.)

HARRY'S HURTING HEART Harry is feeling *"stretched across two universes."* No better person to explain how that feels than Lyra from *His Dark Materials* (you have it on your List).

WHERE HARRY'S HEAD IS One question HP Sleuths might want to contemplate is: what happens to Harry when the hurt and all the emotion goes away? What will be his state of mind, and what about all the open questions about his future that are left over from Book 5? Will he be sharing the knowledge of his disturbing destiny with anyone else or not? What awaits the little man who lived?

PLAN B According to the final chapter, we are assuredly headed for war. Is it going to be an all-out battle like *Star Wars'* "Attack of the Clones" or *The Lord of the Rings'* battle of all Middle Earth? When your cover is blown, your psychological war starts to break down, and you missed the chance to discover the secret of knocking off the only kid who can stop you, *what do you do*? HP Sleuths should think about that as you search for clues in Book 5.

Attention: HP Super Sleuth Trainees

You have a huge mission. You should now be aware that *you haven't even begun* to read Book 5. You will have many, many months of exciting sleuthing and discoveries. (Yippee!)

Our sleuthing radar is receiving a lot of interference from intentional jamming. We already know that J.K.R. is devious. As Game Master, she has been upping the level of difficulty with each book. Additionally, in the first four books, it was a bit easier to spot a subtle guppy clue next to a whale of a red herring. Book 5, however, contains what looks like red herrings, but are really all a peck of stealth clues, themselves. There appear to be least three (and that's conservative) major sub-plots going on in Book 5 that have yet to be revealed!

Dig your HP Sleuth Supplies out of your trunks and grab your nets because...

SNARK HUNTING SEASON IS NOW OPEN!

2s, 4s, 5s,10s, 12s
    9 of 10, 14s
Across, Crossing
Automatic (actions)
Babies, Calves,
    Babytalk
Balance, Measure
Bark, Barking
Bells, Rings,
    Tones
Bolts, Padlocks,
    Chains
Brains, Minds
Bubbles, Balloons,
Ceiling
Chairs
Circles, Round,
    Wheels
Color (pink, blue,
    orange, silver)
Cracking

Crosses
Doors, Corridors
Dreaming
Ducking
Ears (hurt)
Eggs
Eyes (bulging,
    black, hurt)
Frogs, Toads
Glass
Grims
Growing, Swelling
Hands, Claws (hurt)
Hats & Socks, Wool
Heads (severed,
    Missing)
Hearts
Hems & Skirts
Horns
Hot/Cold,
    Flame/Freezing

Jumping/Falling
    Back
Kings, Rooks, Crowns
Knees
Legs/Feet (many)
Levitating, Midair,
    Soar
Mad, Nuts
March
Moon, Planets (Luna,
    Phases, Umbra)
Mouse, Mice
Mouths (open)
Muttering, Mumbling
Necks
Noises, Screeching
Noses (hurt)
Pairs, Doubles, Mate
Pies
Pipes
Pounding, Hammer

Regurgitating
Rubbish
Sharp, Edge, Poking
Silence, Muffle
Sliding, Sinking
Spindly, Spidery
Spots, Dots, Ink
Stinking, Smells
Stone
Stubby, Stump
Tableware
Tails, Queues
Toilets, Dung
Towers
Trunk, Chest, Tree
Turns (left, right)
Twisted, Coiling
Upside-down
Vanishing
Water, Rain, Mist

Please note: *In order to print your pop-outs, we had to rush the list out early. So, Reference Cards are missing: Balance/Measure, Ceiling, Claws, Horns, Glass, Planets, Rubbish, and Noises/Screeching, plus "Hems & Skirts" is out of order.*